THE
HAND
OF THE
SORCERER

The Hand of the Sorcerer is the fourth and final book
in Stephen Brooke's fantasy epic, Donzalo's Destiny,
following the events in The Song of the Sword,
The Shadow of Asak, and The Sign of the Arrow.

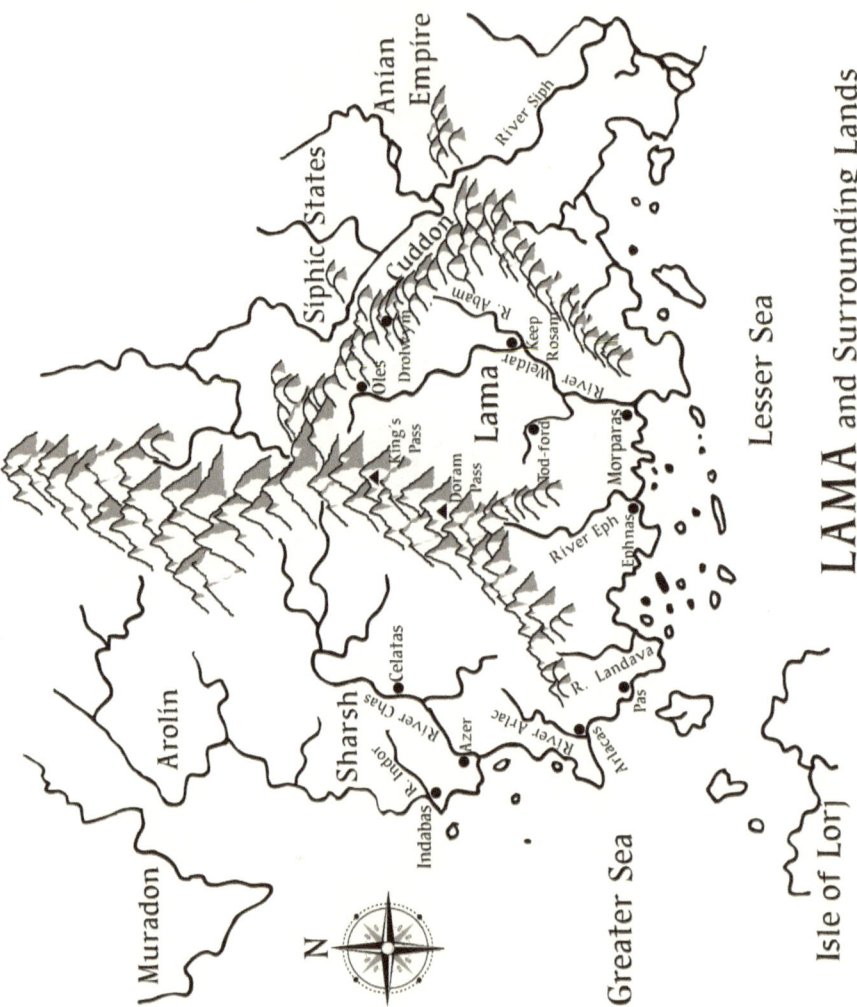

LAMA and Surrounding Lands

THE HAND OF THE SORCERER

STEPHEN BROOKE

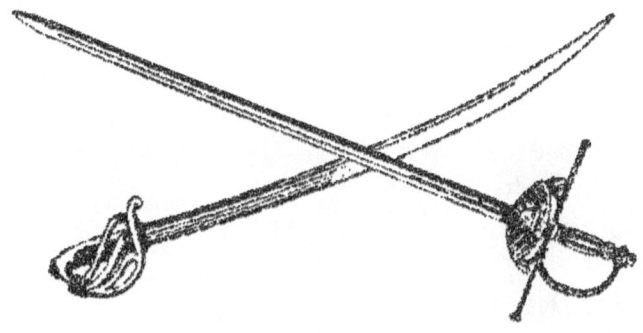

Arachis Press 2014

Whom do you serve?

The Hand of the Sorcerer
©2014 Stephen Brooke

ISBN 978-1-937745-17-2

Arachis Press
4803 Peanut Road
Graceville, FL 32440
http://arachispress.com

The Donzalo's Destiny epic fantasy
by Stephen Brooke consists of four books:
I. The Song of the Sword
II. The Shadow of Ask
III. The Sign of the Arrow
IV. The Hand of the Sorcerer

OF BROTHERS: THE NINTH TALE

1

First came the wild man, shooting sparks from both hands. "Make way! Make way!" he shouted. He lifted his thickly bearded face to the summer sky and howled.

All wrapped in the pelts of animals was he. "The hides protect him from his fireworks," whispered Donzalo to his companions. They seemed mostly those of coyotes.

Behind him came the procession, players of fife, beaters of drum, revelers of both genders and all ages.

This was all new to Habidros, who had seen no such spectacle either in the Siphic cities nor his Cuddonian homeland. His brothers, being more traveled, knew how Lamans celebrated the Feast of Plenty.

"They do this better at your home, Donni," said Guesare.

Galaro nodded agreement. "They haven't the money nor the people for it here. Tod-ford is no more than an overgrown village. Still," he continued, "there will be profits to be made this afternoon and, aye, all the night. I'd best back to my men."

Though Count Orgelo's seat was, indeed, little more than a village, folk from all over County Arvaram, as well as neighboring principalities, had gathered for the festival. Galaro and his band of merchants would do good business tonight and on the morrow.

As the Cuddonian trader exited, the Queen of Plenty entered. Two more wild men accompanied her, armed with great cudgels.

"It's Lenasha," said Habidros, smiling for no apparent reason.

"I've no doubt Orgelo arranged for her coronation," observed Guesare. "Now the question is, whom will she name as her King?" He gave Donzalo a sidelong look. "I would suspect he hopes it to be you, Donni."

Count Orgelo's niece walked through the crowd, holding a crown of grape leaves in her large and rather calloused hands. Her gown was all of green and she herself wore a chaplet of wildflowers. Donzalo admitted to himself that the tall young woman, whom he was used to seeing in dusty riding outfits, looked very much a queen this day.

Right to their group she came. "I name you the King of Abundance — Sir Habidros!" she proclaimed, placing the crown on that knight's head.

Habidros only smiled all the more broadly, and perhaps, some would say, foolishly, as he accompanied his Queen to their thrones.

~ ~ ~

"You must learn to ride a horse properly. Many things may be done sidesaddle, but swinging a sword is not one of them."

Fachalana felt she just might be able to prove her friend wrong about that.

"I think I ride quite well this way," she sniffed, even while recognizing that Ansa was right — straddling her mount would be more practical, despite all her years of training otherwise.

"As well as anyone I've seen sitting sideways," agreed the Anian, "not that *that* counts for much."

"Shall I wear pants like you, Maresta?" asked Lady Fachalana, taking care to use her friend's pseudonym. "If I must ride like a man perhaps I should look like one as well!"

"Do I look like a man?" laughed her slender companion. "I suppose I might pass as a boy, on stage."

Fachalana glanced at the woman riding beside her. Since she had cropped her hair short to remove the dark-dyed ends, Ansa did appear rather boyish. "We shall have such a part written especially for you," she declared.

Then, a thought came to her. Fachalana was given to moments of inspiration, some of which actually made sense. "We could both pose as men if we chose to ride back into Lama. What better disguise?"

Ansa looked to her friend with surprise and then slowly nodded. "A most excellent idea, Lana. We may make a spy of you yet.

"But all the more reason to learn to ride astraddle. We shall fit you out with a proper saddle when we return to the stables."

~ ~ ~

This little patch of land, known as the Laman March, was the only place where the kingdom of Sharsh extended eastward beyond the mountains. Only four leagues was its width where it lay in the foothills below Mountain Keep, and twice that was its length.

Here Lareth was mustering a small army, a few hundred men, and a larger force at the keep, should they be needed. More might alarm the counts of Lama and might prove unwieldy if called upon to ride into the wide valley of the Weldar.

Nonetheless, men were also being mobilized on the other side of the mountains, in Sharsh, ready at both the King's Pass and that of Dor to invade in much larger numbers. King Lareth prayed to Jov and to any other gods that might be listening that such would be unnecessary.

Indeed, if all went well the men he had already sent secretly into Lama could be sufficient, the two-score Sir Blen had led into the south and twice that number the king had sent, a few at a time, to assemble in the lands of Count Dordos.

He rode now up into the mountains, returning to Mountain Keep. It could not be seen until one was almost upon it, hidden by a spur of the Zadcelam, around which wound the Royal Road. Lareth rode and pondered.

There had been another attempt on his son's life. Perhaps he should have ordered him back to the capital rather than only suggesting it. But then, the boy was probably as safe there at Grenethas, especially under the watchful eye of Lady Fachalana and her friends. He would have to learn more of this young fellow Pol — Sir Pol, now — who had stopped the latest would-be assassin.

Lareth sighed. He had been guilty of sending assassins to murder another man's son himself. Indeed, much of the current situation stemmed from those actions. To think that the boy he had wished dead was the father of the king's own grandson!

That his beloved daughter was an adulteress bothered him not one bit. The younger brother was obviously a much finer man than the husband with whom he and diplomacy had burdened her.

But it most definitely complicated things.

~ ~ ~

The nearby calls of a moorcock awakened Perdos. He was reminded of the clucking chickens in his family's yard, long ago. He should be feeding them or Father would be angry.

No, Father was dead these many years. The knight shook off the remainder of his sleep and rose. His blanket was wet with the fogs rising from the Weldar, close at hand.

Where now? Since his slaying of the mercenary Sojel, he had been uncertain of his course. Perdos had relieved himself of a great burden of hatred with that slaying.

Another might have said that Perdos had seen his father in the man he had killed. Perdos would have claimed that he just despised anyone who mistreated women. Be that as it may, he still sought vengeance on the minstrel Guesare.

That braying came from cormorants, didn't it? They sounded like a herd of asses. Too bad they weren't — donkeys could be turned into ready money. Perdos had found the presence of mind, following their clash, to gather the horses of Sojel and his two henchmen and use them to increase his supply of cash. There was a very practical businessman somewhere inside Sir Perdos.

He hated Guesare, yes, but it was not the same. He no longer desired simply to kill the man; no, he saw it now as a matter of honor, of vendetta, against an opponent he had come grudgingly to respect. Perdos would meet the Cuddonian fairly one of these days, sword against sword, and settle their quarrel. Sojel, he would have knifed from behind and felt no qualms.

Yet he was glad to have seen the man's face, before he severed head from body.

The Cuddonians were still up in County Arvaram. They wouldn't stay forever. He could linger here a while longer, pick up what news came along the road, and wait his chance.

~ ~ ~

"I had hoped she would name you, Donni," the count lamented. "Sir Habidros is a fine fellow but he is far too much like my son!"

"I think Habi wishes to leave my service and enter yours," said Donzalo.

"And Sir Copago wishes to do the opposite," replied Orgelo. "I am not opposed to the idea. Habidros is well suited to life in the saddle."

"As is your niece, my lord," remarked the young knight.

Orgelo rarely laughed aloud, as he did not like to show his missing teeth, victims of accident and of time, but now he did. "Indeed she is, my boy! I would have hoped for a higher match for her." He paused to glance meaningfully at Donzalo. "But if your cousin asks for Lenasha's hand — and she is willing — I think I would say yes."

"We should have suspected something as much time as those two spent riding together," observed Donzalo.

"What of her father?" he asked. Donzalo had heard nothing of her parents.

"Long dead." The count sighed. "He was, as you, a younger son of a count of Lama. Unlike you, he was a fool and wastrel and was murdered in a brothel. I am the girl's guardian.

"She has grown up here, learning more of horsemanship than of etiquette. Her mother," he added with a shrug, "devotes herself to religion.

"It appears the festivities of this night are winding down at last. I think I will to my bed."

"Dawn is as good a time as any, my lord," replied Donzalo.

2

His hound Sojel had served him well.

Now he was gone. So be it. The man had wrought his own undoing.

"What name has the second-in-command?" Radal asked the messenger.

"Dovolo, my lord," answered the man, a nondescript ruffian who carried a bad odor about with himself.

"Do you know if he can read?"

The man shook his head uncertainly. "Not mine to ask, sir."

Radal approved of such an attitude, in general. "Well, I'm sure somebody there can read my messages to him, even if he is unlettered. Whoever wrote this, perhaps." He held up the scrap of paper he had been holding.

The scoundrel seemed to have no answer to that. Radal shrugged and continued.

"You shall bear my message back to this Dovolo, confirming him as my new sergeant." Though he would now have to take more of a hand himself, the sorcerer recognized. "It will require some time. Go rest yourself." He turned from the man without further word and entered the ruined keep which served temporarily as his headquarters.

Who would have thought such a seeming fool as Perdos could be Sojel's bane? If Radal had known the knight were so capable he might not have thrown him aside, a tool that was no longer of use.

Perhaps the lesson here was to destroy such used tools, lest another pick them up.

Lord Radal wished he could pass such lessons on to the one person for whom he most cared now, his daughter Fachalana. He had begun to suspect that others protected her when she fled from his attempts at contact, shielded her from his link in some place he could not see. Did she guess that she had such guardians?

If he could discover who they were, he might be able to move against them. But there were other concerns requiring his attention now.

He might not be able to reach the mind of Fachalana but there was another, his spy in County Rosam, with whom he could form a link. The boy was of little talent but he would serve Radal's needs.

Benawis! he called.

~ ~ ~

What bow has set me to this futile flight,
Has sent me arcing to your armored heart?
Dare I trace the journey of that dart
To some willful archer of the night,

Some jokester god who, laughing, took his aim
At a mark no man might penetrate,
Leaving me to curse both love and fate?
No, I will myself take all the blame

And know I was a fool, as are men all,
For we choose to fly and, spent, must fall.

"The legate wrote that?" asked Sir Pol.

"It certainly sounds like him," opined Fachalana. She strongly suspected that the sentiments in the piece were directed toward their friend Lomela. He would always love his princess, even were he to wed the Lady Fachalana. "Is that his second book of poems, Modi?"

Prince Modareth nodded. "That it is, Lana. I fear my father is keeping him too busy to compose a third."

"Not to mention Fachalana giving him the task of writing a play for her," added Ansa.

"I have seen him at work on it, my ladies," Pol said, "pacing back and forth and reciting the lines he had written. Who is this Nordoc, anyway?"

"A king in Lorj, wasn't he?" hazarded Princess Carrana. "You are the scholar, Husband."

When no one else showed interest in taking on the subject, the prince sighed and spoke. Modareth was not greatly enamored of giving lectures.

"It was near eight centuries ago, on the Isle of Lorj, that Nordoc and Oemse lived. At that time, most of eastern Lorj was ruled by the Caram Empire."

"Cars was their capital, wasn't it?" asked Fachalana.

"Yes, but it was pronounced Caras then. The Lorjans have lately taken to dropping some of their vowels.

"Anyway, the Caram Emperors had been mighty and had also spread the Kamatian religion through their realm."

"Kamatianism drove their conquests, I have read," said Ansa.

Modareth nodded. "But the empire had grown weak and was torn by civil wars. That was when the northern provinces, subjugated lands which included the Coradean nation, rose up in rebellion. One of the growing powers that bordered the empire sent the mercenary captain Nordoc with his company to aid the uprising.

"Naturally, they hoped to bring the area under their sway in time or, at least, to discomfit and weaken the Caram without committing any of their own troops."

"Thus Oemse's Question," said Fachalana.

"Oh, I know that," piped up Carrana. "*And whom do you serve, Captain Nordoc?*"

There were smiles all around. "Yes, my wife. Nordoc stopped in one of the towns and asked them if they would continue to serve the Caram Empire. That is when the young rebel leader Oemse stepped forward and posed her famous question.

"And that is when Captain Nordoc decided to quit his paymasters and become his own man," Modareth concluded. Or so he thought.

"And became a king, sir?" asked Pol. 'King Nordoc' was the title of a well-known play, after all.

"Indeed. He grabbed a goodly portion of those northern provinces as his own and named his kingdom Oemsebe in honor of the woman who had shown him his destiny."

"And whom he loved," Fachalana added. "Nordoc married her

but she was taken by the Caram troops and executed. That is the tragedy that Jobareth is writing."

"Tragic it might have been," was the prince's reply, "but it did not prevent Nordoc from taking several wives later on and fathering many unruly heirs.

"In time, Cel Oemsebe — which most called by its older name of the Northing Kingdom — was absorbed into the growing Coradean Empire."

He smiled benignly. "But the history of the Northing War is another lesson, children."

"Sir?" asked Pol. He seemed uncertain but went on. "Are there books I might read? That tell of these things?"

Modareth gestured toward the towering shelves that lined one side of the room. "I'll show you some, Sir Pol. We both may be doing more reading once the ladies are on the road."

"You are going to give us our passports, Modareth?" asked Facha-lana.

"Yes, both the real ones and the false. I hope you two know what you are doing."

Pol had known nothing of this. "You are leaving, my ladies?"

Ansa answered. "We intend to sneak back into Lama and make sure Princess Lomela and Jobareth are safe and well." And Donzalo, too, she added to herself. "We needed passports both as ourselves and as, um, someone else." Of course, Ansa's legitimate passport would have her name as Maresta — few knew her true identity.

The young knight nodded. It was not his to question their motives. But he thought he should speak of another matter.

"I do not trust the legate's secretary, Benawis," he stated outright. "I would advise that you do not, as well."

~ ~ ~

"Count Daboreth looks much like your brother," remarked Galaro, "if your brother spent his days in the saddle."

Donzalo nodded absentmindedly. He had noted Daboreth's family resemblance. "Bolos does take after our mother's people." The young knight barely remembered his mother and, somewhere along the line, her loss had become mingled with that of his Jola.

"It will take the better part of two days to reach Dabbi's place. Are you certain you wish to come?"

"I want to see this brimstone. My men can sit here for a week. Business should be good enough." Galaro looked into his young companion's eyes. "And are you certain you will not come south with us then?"

"I think not," came the answer, yet Donzalo seemed uncertain.

He has no place to truly call a home now, thought Galaro. Why shouldn't he travel south with me, and Guesare, as well? There are many opportunities for a man such as he in the south.

"Here comes Orgelo," said Donzalo. Their host was flanked by Copago and Habidros.

"Greetings, my lord," said Galaro to Count Orgelo. "So, who is coming and who is staying?"

"I shall remain," spoke Habidros. "Sorry to leave you, Donni, but, well — you know why I stay. Between Guesare and Sir Copago and, yes, my oversize brother here, you will be well guarded."

Donzalo embraced his cousin and erstwhile bodyguard, whispering in his ear, "I expect an invitation to the wedding."

"Sir Habidros can teach my men much," Orgelo said. He turned to Copago. "It seems we were not able to become a home for you, my boy. I am sorry for that."

"My lord, I thank you for allowing me to serve for a while."

"Ah, Sir Copago, ever the steady one, aren't you? I know you did not enjoy riding with my son day after day." Orgelo smiled. "Even I could not take that much of him!"

He spoke then to Donzalo. "I am hearing unsettling things out of County Rosam. Be careful and know that we, too, are keeping an eye on happenings there. If need be, my men are ready to ride."

Guesare and Daboreth had strolled up to the small group. "Are *we* ready to ride?" asked the minstrel, in mock impatience.

"I believe we are," replied Sir Copago, and then added, allowing just a touch of wistfulness to enter his voice, "I wonder if the peaches are ripening back in County Rosam."

~ ~ ~

Count Mussago looked again at the message from Daboreth, his neighbor to the south. Borrago's son? He had no quarrels with County Rosam and didn't really care much, one way or the other, about Daboreth either. Certainly he would give them safe passage.

In fact, he should invite them to visit here. His secretary could write something for him to sign.

Mussago reached down and stroked the dog beside his chair. Mussago had a great love for dogs and was noted as a breeder. Indeed, he had given one to little Ros Rosam on his naming day. He wondered how it was doing these days. It should be fully grown by now, physically, even if still a playful puppy in many ways.

The count scratched at his chin with a plump hand. Those Sharshite soldiers he was letting camp on his land should know of this too. Didn't they have something to do with the Rosam? He must have the secretary send notice to Sir Blen, as well.

3

Benawis served Lord Radal.

But to serve Lord Radal was surely to serve himself. To serve himself was always the first goal of the young scholar.

Even before the lord councilor gave him this post as secretary to Nafal, Benawis had served. That day he had waited on a garden bench outside Radal's tall doors, the sorcerer had felt the young man's latent powers as his daydreams had, quite unconsciously, carried him into other worlds, recognized that he, untutored boy though he be, possessed talent.

He had learned from the great sorcerer. So what if he had not the natural gifts of a Radal? Any knowledge, any skill, could be used to further his own needs.

And all men had needs. Those who claimed that they did not put those needs foremost were liars. The gods, if they existed, would understand the appetites of men. Had they not provided the night so we might tend to them?

Radal had asked only of news at the keep, but Benawis sensed that he meant soon to act. Perhaps he would aid the dark lord with his schemes; perhaps he would not. It was widely known now that the man was out of favor.

It would depend on how he felt about it at the time — and where his own good lay.

His thoughts lingered for some time on Radal's daughter, the Lady Fachalana. She was a prize for which he might risk much, beautiful and full of power. Benawis knew without asking that the sorcerer would not hear of such a thing; indeed, it would be worth his life to suggest it.

It was good that Lord Radal had taught him to cloak his own power or she might have found him out. The time might come when Benawis would be able to use that power to take what he desired.

~ ~ ~

A man hung from the gibbet by the road.

"It is our would-be assassin," said Ansa, as calmly as possible.

Ansa had seen more of death than she liked to admit but its presence shook her still. She hoped it always would.

Her companion briefly looked up at the hanged man and then quickly away, urging her horse forward. Lady Fachalana had her own memories of a death that haunted her at times.

"A Mur, they said. Do you think Mura had anything to do with this?"

"I would doubt it. What would the Muram emperor care who sat the throne of Sharsh?" asked the Anian. "Many Muram soldiers turned mercenary after your king's last war with them."

"Your people have warred with them too, haven't they?"

"Border skirmishes in the disputed territories north of Lama. We never pressed into the Muram homeland." Ansa was feeling more herself now that they were well past the gallows. "And since, we have withdrawn from that area altogether."

"I suspect our Pol has his portion of Muram blood, considering where he was born. It has not been long since Arolin was a part of their empire."

"Ha, do not say that to him!" warned Ansa. Both knew of his hatred of the Mura and the reasons for it. "He doesn't look it, anyway."

"You look rather Anian today," remarked Fachalana. "I do hope you intend to change out of those trousers before we reach the pass."

"And you need better conceal that pigtail," her friend replied. The noblewoman had pulled her long hair back into a tight braid that she had tucked into the collar of her leather jerkin. A voluminous beret did not completely hide it.

"A helmet will cover it," Fachalana said.

"We can't go armored all the time, even if it does best hide our forms."

The Sharshite looked her companion over. "You look every bit the boy you pretend to be. A rather fearsome boy, too, with that bow." Ansa wore a recurved bow of the eastern sort on her back.

17

"And your height is an asset to your deception," said Ansa. "You are taller than many a soldier we have seen on the road today."

"There are quite a few, aren't there? Something must be going on."

"No doubt, Lana, no doubt. But we can't expect the king to tell us everything."

~ ~ ~

That her father was behind this, the Lady Mara was most certain.

Or, more properly, the circle of powerful ministers who surrounded the emperor. They were the true rulers of Partanaca, the Imperial Council. It was they who had sent her to this marriage in Sharsh.

Not that she minded that. It was a good marriage as such political matches go. She and Prince Gawis were fond enough of each other, even if not in love.

Yet her marriage to the heir to the throne of Sharsh was at the root of this trouble. That same council, undoubtedly, had sent assassins against his younger brother.

She looked at that heir, seated in a comfortable chair in the corner of her chambers. He was pulling on his soft leather boots.

The beginnings of a beard, darker than his straw-colored thatch of hair, framed the boyish face. Gawis would look good with a beard, she thought. People might even take him more seriously.

"Your brother will come back to the capital, you think?"

Gawis looked up from his lacing. "Father did not order it. And it is still very hot here." He smiled at his wife. "Would that we could go to the mountains for a month."

He considered that thought for a moment. "You and the girls should get out of Celatas until the autumn. There are many villas in the hills that would welcome you."

"You know I love the heat of summer, Husband." Lady Mara was a child of the hot southern isles. "But it might be good for the children." She laughed at a sudden thought. "Your brother would be most surprised if we showed up at his door!"

18

Gawis laughed with her. "I should like to see his face."

"Perhaps I and the girls will go down to the shore for a time."

The prince nodded. The sea was in his wife's blood. It would do her good to stay a while by its side. "An excellent idea, my dear. Just remember me now and again, sweltering here and attending to my princely duties."

~ ~ ~

"Have you seen the mines of Lorj, Sir Galaro?"

"No, but I know those on Ussan." Ussan was the largest of the isles that lay between Lorj and the mainland. "If there be brimstone there and brimstone here, then it would not be surprising to find it in the lands that lie between, would it?"

"Orgelo's holdings, you mean?" asked Daboreth.

"Aye, and all the south-lands beyond County Arvaram. Though I have traversed that area many times and seen none."

"Let us hope Orgelo never sees any either," stated Donzalo, "or all this might be in vain."

The group gathered around the big table murmured their agreement.

"Have *we* seen enough?" asked Guesare. "Or need we spend more time looking at rocks?"

Sir Copago spoke. "We have seen quite enough. Now is the time for making plans."

"My plan shall be to ride back to Orgelo's in the morning, I and my man," said Galaro. "All I can do is wish you luck at this time. And thank my host for his hospitality," he added, with a nod toward Count Daboreth.

"It was my pleasure, Sir Galaro. Do bring those bagpipes your brother so maligns should you visit again."

"That I shall, my lord!"

"We should leave soon, as well, " said Copago. "What plans we intend for this brimstone we had best make now."

All eyes at the table turned toward Donzalo. Well, it was my idea, he told himself.

"The actual making of the gunpowder is easy enough — simply mix the proper ingredients in their proper proportions. A central location, perhaps near Ros-town or even Todmouth, might be the best place to do that. The making of the ingredients will prove more difficult." The young knight paused so his comrades might speak. None did.

"Right here is our best source of brimstone. It can be refined and carted to whatever location we decide upon. It is not," he continued, "the ideal place for the rest of it, but could possibly serve."

"What forest remains in these parts is sparse," observed Copago. "The supply of charcoal would run short quickly."

"And fires are needed to burn and refine the brimstone, as well," said Donzalo. "Best the charcoal be made upriver, where wood is plentiful."

"We could always bring it down from the mountains."

"Yes, Dabbi, it would take a great deal of effort but that is an alternative."

The count nodded his agreement. He understood this.

"And then there is the saltpeter," said Sir Copago. "If Count Daboreth's cattle were more confined that might not be so difficult to obtain. But they are scattered across this sparse countryside."

"Yes," agreed Donzalo. "Again, it could be done here but it is not the most practical way. I would really like to get at those caves filled with bat droppings back home."

"That is not a statement I ever expected to hear from you, " said Guesare. "Nor any other man, for that matter."

"I have come to expect the unexpected about here, lately," laughed Daboreth. "To the unexpected!" he toasted, raising his cup.

"The unexpected!" came from all around the table.

"I think," Guesare then said, "that we should spend the next day or two helping our friend Daboreth and his men set up their refinery. It is simple enough a process." The minstrel was the only one of the group who had ever actually seen it done. "That accomplished, we can be on our way and leave further plans wait."

Donzalo nodded. He knew that they looked to him for decisions, even though he was the youngest and least experienced of them all.

"So, this Count Mussago wishes us to visit his keep?" he asked. "Is it far out of our way?"

"Hardly at all," replied Daboreth, "and he and Count Dordos control much of the road between Doram Pass and the Weldar. It would be good to have him as your friend.

"In fact, he invited me as well so I shall accompany you!"

4

"As anticipated, sir, the man knew nothing beyond the name of he who hired him." The captain looked up from his report. "Which was, of course, a false name."

"Of course," came Modareth's even reply.

"None the less, we were able to learn something of this paymaster. He used a different name at the inn here in town — um, yes, a Marin Sorgovam," he said, finding it on the page. "I have no doubt, my lord, that it is false as well."

The prince tried to contain himself — he had intended to remain stern and severe throughout this interview — but broke out in laughter.

"False indeed, Captain. Marin Sorgovam was an ancient emperor of the Coradeans."

"It would seem, my lord, that your enemy has a sense of humor." This came from the ever-present Sir Pol. Pol took his duties as body-guard seriously, even to sleeping on the threshold of his prince's bedchamber.

"And some learning," said Modareth.

"Might it be intended as a taunt, sir?" asked the captain.

"It may well be. Though had I been slain, I do not know who might have appreciated it."

The man himself, enjoying his private joke, thought Pol. "Is there aught else on the fellow?" he asked.

"A general description only, Sir Pol." The captain slightly resented this young fellow who had become the prince's favorite and constant companion. He turned back to his master. "My lord, we have sent couriers to all the nearby towns to keep an eye out for him."

"An eye out for a nondescript man with a false name?" asked Pol.

The captain resented the knight more than slightly now. "Well, sir, we know that he always wore a long tunic — gray, most say — and that he turned up his nose at the local wine." With a chuckle, he added, "Everyone remembered that detail."

"Good enough," said Prince Modareth. "Thank you, Captain." That was a signal for the soldier to leave, which he did.

"Sir," said Pol, "do you think that might be the sorcerer of whom the Lady Fachalana told us?" They had heard Fachalana's tale of the dreams that brought her to both the prince's door and his rescue, and of her father's conjectures about them.

Modareth shrugged. "It is possible. Whoever the man is, he thinks himself most clever."

"Yes, my lord, the name. The belief in their own cleverness may trip such men up." Sir Pol stood silently for a few moments. "Are we going to head back to Celatas?"

Modareth rose from behind his desk and walked to the wide doors, open to the cool evening air. The gardens here looked far better than when he and Carrana had arrived, didn't they? "I think so, Pol. Maybe in a week or two. With my wife's pregnancy it would be best to travel sooner rather than later. You have never been to the capital, have you?"

"No, sir, I have not. I am not sure how I will fit into your household there."

"As you do here, if you wish. Or would you rather be back to soldiering, I am sure my father would appoint you to almost any post you desire."

"I've no great love of being a soldier, sir. I do wonder if I should be keeping an eye on the ladies. No one else is." He shook his head, remembering that Blen had asked him to watch over them. "Couldn't you have ordered them not to go?"

"Pol, once Fachalana has set her mind to something, no one can prevent her. She and Maresta will follow their own road for now.

"You took on their pair of servants as your personal retainers, didn't you? Best you let them know we're going to be on the road soon as well."

~ ~ ~

Lady Thara had listened patiently to her husband's reading of the letter. "What will Bolos think of all this?" she asked then.

"He may not like it but he can not object to me making Sir

Copago my master of arms. After all," he pointed out, "I did give him my own when he asked for him."

Thara nodded. "We must send Corgos his wife soon, before travel becomes unwise." That Tiana was pregnant had become common knowledge.

"As soon as Copago is here to take charge, I shall go visit our nephew and convey the lady to her husband." Sir Paren placed the missive on the polished wooden table between them. It had been crafted right here at his manor from one of the great poplars, the tallest trees in the forests that lay about the estate. "I suspect that Donzalo and Guesare will also wish to accompany me."

"I hope that Donzalo chooses to return with you. He should cease his wandering." Thara knew her husband agreed with that thought. "I should inform Dame Janona of her husband's coming."

"There was a separate letter for her, from Sir Copago. She would know of it by now."

"And his mother as well, no doubt." Lady Thara seemed briefly miffed that she could not bear such happy news to her friends. Then she brightened. "At least I can tell Tiana!"

"Feel free to do so, Wife," said Paren. "Would that the news that comes out of Keep Rosam were as good."

By all accounts, Bolos had fallen back into his ways as a drunkard and everywhere saw plots against him. Maybe he could settle the man down. Whom might he trust if not his old uncle?

"And let us hope that our travelers do not tarry overmuch along the way."

~ ~ ~

"Jan and Saj we are," stated Ansa in a gruff tone. "Oh, you did that so well, Lana!"

"You'd best use my man-name from now on," warned Fachalana, "even in private. And," she added, "don't be impertinent toward your betters, boy."

"Oh, of course. I know my spy-craft, Sir Jan. Or is it stage-craft?"

"They feel much the same to me."

"I suppose they are," mused Ansa. She had practiced both long and knew how similar they could be. "A rider ahead."

"He seems to be sitting his horse and waiting."

Ansa knew immediately who it was that awaited them here on the road up to Doram Pass. Had his message not reached her at Grenethas, saying to watch for him?

But she would let him play this encounter as he wished and say nothing to her companion.

Fachalana raised a hand in greeting to the stranger. The face beneath the fur cap seemed vaguely familiar, but she knew she had never met this man.

"Hail, travelers!" called he.

"Greetings, sir," she responded, her voice as low as she could manage. Maybe it should have more gravel to it? "I be Sir Jan, a knight of Sharsh."

"Greetings to you, Sir Jan." The man then leered at Ansa, saying, "Your esquire is quite a pretty boy. Would you sell him to me?"

"What?" The astounded noblewoman put her hand to her sword hilt. Furthering her confusion, both the stranger and her companion burst into laughter.

"Let me introduce you to my brother Oder," said Ansa. Of her brother she asked, "Didn't we fool you at all?"

"How could I not recognize my own sister? Still," he said, looking the two over, "not bad at all. A rather ruffianly pair, I would say."

Fachalana did not like the idea that she looked a ruffian. That had not been been at all her intention! "Sir Oder, surely you recognize a gentleman when you see one," she said in haughty tones. All three shared in the laughter this time.

"If I might," said Oder, "I would suggest a hood and cowl, my lady. 'Tis a bit old-fashioned but many fighting men still wear them beneath their helms."

Ansa nodded her agreement. "You are right, Oder. It would hide many tell-tales."

"I've one in my bags, my ladies. Or gentlemen, if you prefer to remain in character. Jan and Saj, eh? Such common names may seem a wise choice but they can also arouse suspicions.

"There is a shelter back that way a bit where we might speak of many things." He gestured in the direction toward which they had been traveling. "Let us stop there a while."

The shelter was only a few minutes away, a shallow cave at the base of a cliff overhanging their road. There were no other travelers sharing it this early in the day.

"On the morrow, you should cross over the divide," said Oder, "and begin your descent toward Lama. The way is long and rough but not so steep as on this side."

"And where are you going, Sir Oder?" asked Fachalana.

"It's not polite to ask such things of a spy," warned Ansa.

"At worst, he will only lie to me," was her friend's retort. Ansa knew her brother was capable of far worse things than lying but spoke not.

"I shall not lie today, my lady," replied the spy-master, chewing on a bit of the bread and cheese they shared. "We are alarmed by some of the goings-on in Sharsh and, in particular, the attempts on the life of your friend, the prince. I will spend but a few days with my agents there so I may report."

"What does the Anian Empire care about Prince Modareth?"

"Little, in truth. It is the ambitions of Partanaca that concern us. That is all I have to say on that.

"But I will cross back into Lama soon, whether by Doram Pass or the secret ways I know. We may meet again, my ladies, as you go about whatever mission you have set yourself.

"Of course, it would not be polite to ask two so lovely spies about such things."

~ ~ ~

Radal was not sure when he had first heard the voice of Darkness, but it had come with forgiveness for all the thoughts, all the desires, his mother had told him were sins. They are nothing, said Darkness, and her voice was as soft winds of night.

26

She whispered to him that the gods were only little things and would perish as surely as men. Then only she in her primal majesty would remain. Naught else would matter.

The sorcerer had a small obsidian figure he had found as a boy, half-buried in the clay by the river. His father, the tall stern soldier, had told him it was only a chess piece someone had lost but he knew that it was *she*, come to him so he might worship.

That figurine resided now in distant Celatas, on a shelf in his study. Perhaps it had been but a lost gaming piece. Perhaps it had no power other than that he gave it.

Darkness, the goddess of that unhappy boy, Radal now knew as a manifestation of the Great Void in our world. The Void was indifferent to all existence. It did not even hate, being empty of all things. But Darkness hated, as had Radal.

He would serve her always and her father, Death — Asak, as the Kamatians named him, and the Ildin before them. Someday, soon probably, Asak would come and give him his gift of peace, of extinction. He would be with his goddess.

Until then he would serve her, though she asked nothing of men.

Radal remembered still the hymn the boy had composed in her honor, that he had intoned before his little obsidian idol.

Darkness, Asak's eldest child,
Lady of the Lifeless Lands,
on your carved ebon throne,
scatter Time's unnumbered sands.

Wisdom comes as nightmare runes,
written on the lids of eyes
that beheld you, vast and still,
ere stars rose in ancient skies.

All the children of the day,
generations raised in light,

shrink from the Abyss's gaze,
waste and wither in your sight.

Darkness, born of endless Void,
Goddess to the men of old,
reign as Queen of endless realms,
worlds where all things grow cold.

Radal smiled thinly at the memory and, with a sigh, turned to his work. He must soon act, and decisively. Then let things be as they would be, knowing that Darkness did not listen to prayers.

5

"Bolos has banished the boy's dog?" Count Mussago pursed his lips and shook his head. He looked as if he might have said many things about Bolos but had thought better of it.

Dogs had greeted them at the count's door. Many dogs. Most were white and of a uniform size and shape, not overly large, and well-formed.

"King's brothers and sisters and cousins, I suspect," had been Sir Copago's observation.

Mussago's keep was an unkempt pile of stones well up in the foothills of the Zadcelam and overlooking the road from Doram Pass. The travelers could see it was well placed to control traffic through the mountains.

They had crossed a range of low scrubby hills to reach this county. Here the streams flowed easterly toward the Weldar. South of the hills, in Daboreth's lands, they ran to the Tod and Count Orgelo's dominion.

Donzalo reached a hand down to allow one of the canines to sniff at it. It approved of his scent. Count Mussago approved of anyone his dogs liked.

"If — King, you named him? — King has a good home, I suppose all is well," said the count. "King should also improve the bloodlines about Sir Paren's keep," he added with a chuckle.

"You style them warden dogs, my lord, don't you?" asked Sir Copago.

"Yes, my boy. Smaller than mastiffs but quicker, and large enough to watch and protect."

"There is mastiff in their lineage, I would wager," said Daboreth, "and maybe some of the local herding dogs?"

"You have a good eye, neighbor," replied the stout nobleman. "There are contributions from across the mountains, as well. Now, most of those that I am willing to sell go to Sharsh." The count had thrown a richly decorated if slightly threadbare caftan on over a rough costume any farmer might have worn. He prided himself on not minding dirt on his hands.

"I will, of course, give you letters to allow free use of the road. Dordos will honor them. Three smaller counties lie between my borders and his, and each would otherwise try to charge you tolls for passage.

"See to it, will you?" said Mussago, turning to an aide, "and then bring them to me to sign." To his guests, he said, "Orgelo's passports would not get you far in this neighborhood."

He looked squarely at Count Daboreth and stated, "You should visit here more often, Daboreth. Orgelo may not be the friend you think him."

"I've no illusions about Count Orgelo. But family and geography tie me to him."

"A better road between here and Count Daboreth's hold would help," observed Copago. "You might be surprised at what could come over it."

"Oh? I am forever hearing that I should pay more attention to my roads." The count spoke to an attendant who had entered the room. "Our lunch is ready?"

"Yes, my lord," answered the servant.

"Then let us repair to my dining room, gentlemen. My grand-daughter will be there, Daboreth. You must make her acquaintance!"

~ ~ ~

Jobareth waited patiently.

Young Ros was, in most respects, a very well behaved boy but he detested nap-time. "Why do you bother?" asked the diplomat. "Let the lad have his toys if he does not want to sleep."

Both Lomela and Traspa clearly disapproved of this advice. "Boys his age need their naps," asserted the maid.

"Perhaps the legate could use one as well," said Lady Lomela, with a weary smile.

"Would that the siesta were the custom here as it is back in Sharsh," replied Jobareth. "The Laman summer truly is too hot to be out and about in the midday."

"Jobo!" called the tyke, holding his arms out to Nafal.

30

"I'll not come to your rescue today, young man," replied Jobareth. "It would bring the wrath of Mistress Traspa down upon me."

"You shall have to call her Dame Traspa soon," Lomela said. "The wedding is not that far away."

"If she remembers to call me Legate," responded he, with a slight bow toward Traspa. "Sir Jak is a lucky man."

"I think I am lucky, young sir," said Traspa, her voice quite earnest. "He is a good solid man."

"That he is," affirmed the princess. "He has served well in keeping my husband from harm's way."

"Not Sir Corgos?" asked Jobareth Nafal.

"Corgos is a soldier. He has not the temperament to play nurse-maid, I think." She smiled. "He is most definitely not Copago, taking a personal interest in everything in the keep."

Jobareth nodded. He had seen that the new master of arms seemed to prefer the chain of command.

"Shh," whispered Mistress Traspa. "The little lord has fallen asleep."

~ ~ ~

"Your brother is both minstrel and spy, isn't he?" asked Facha-lana.

Ansa nodded. She was distracted by the view of the great Laman valley extending below them into a distant blue-gray haze. What might these lands hold for them in the days to come?

"Do you know any more of his songs?" persisted the Sharshite as they followed the winding, slowly descending trail. There had been no traffic since a line of pack-mules had passed them earlier in the morning.

"Some," she replied. "They tend to be about strife rather than love. Oder is a warrior at heart." Then she asked, of a sudden, "Did you know that Pol writes poems?"

"Truly? I must ask him to recite when next we see him."

"No need to wait. I can give you one right here."

Lady Fachalana was already aware that her friend possessed a prodigious memory for songs and plays. "How do you come to know it? Has our boy been writing love poems to you?" she asked with a laugh.

"None that I have seen," replied Ansa. "Which does not mean that they do not exist."

Does she hope they do? wondered Fachalana.

"I came upon him scribbling lines in the library," continued the Anian, "and he quite unabashedly asked my opinion of them." She began to recite, her voice clear and musical.

Never trust a poet —
he'll only tell you lies
and pretty bits of nonsense,
pretending to be wise.

The words have all been crafted
to bring tears to your eyes;
he'll beguile your hearts,
he'll seek to hear your sighs.

But, in time, he knows
whatever words he tries,
you'll turn the page and read
some other poet's lies.

"Our Pol is a bit of a cynic, isn't he?"

"I would say a sometimes-disappointed romantic, rather. And he was poking fun at Jobareth's work."

"Hmm, I can see that. It's not really all that good, is it?"

"Nor particularly original. But good enough and he composed it pretty much on the spot, in a minute or two. That would be a considerable gift for one who wrote for the stage rather than books." She was silent for a few moments. "Pol is very smart, you know."

"And ambitious," said Fachalana. "I wonder if Jobareth truly chose him as his man or if he chose Jobareth."

"Well, he is a prince's man now. Who knows where he will go from there?"

~ ~ ~

Many bodies of troops passed him on the road. This made Oder nervous.

Whatever reason there was for their presence was almost certainly more important than the affair he had been sent here to investigate. Of the assassination attempt, and what followed after, the news he had heard from his sister had proven more useful than the reports of his agents.

Ansa was valuable as a spy. Of that there was not the least doubt, and all the more so since she had become the friend of a prince. Yet the Anian spy-master would be happy to see her retire from this life of danger. She should go back to the empire and marry some young nobleman there. Plenty enough of them had vied for her hand before she chose to follow her brother's profession.

Here in Sharsh, he was passing himself off as a merchant out of Lama. His credentials were the finest that might be forged; that was no problem. But there seemed to be a suspicion of Lamans right now. Added to that was a general mistrust of strangers following the attempt on Prince Modareth's life. Oder believed he should leave Sharsh quickly and quietly.

There were ways other than the two great passes to cross the mountains. Longer ways, harder ways, but safer ones, perhaps. Best he get the news that Sharsh was massing troops on the Laman border to his superiors as soon as possible.

He turned his horse onto a little-traveled road that led into the high Zadcelam.

~ ~ ~

The Lady Mara dreamed.

She was in Xose, the city of her birth, and her girls were there with her. But she was no older than they, playing with them on the sand beaches she remembered so well. The water was warm there and the waves gentle. So different from the cold rough surf here on Sharsh's shores!

"Look at my castle," said her oldest daughter, standing over a marvelously sculpted sand edifice. And as she did, it grew larger and the gates opened to her. There was Gawis, waiting for her.

No, his face changed and became that of another, that of a younger man. "Where is my husband?" she asked of him. He only took her hand and led her into a high-vaulted hall. There stood scribe and priest, as they had at her wedding.

"Gawis," she whispered. "Gawis."

He was nowhere.

When the lady awoke she tried to remember the face of the man she was wedding. But it was gone, fled into the shadows of sleep.

Six men had ridden to Count Mussago's castle. Now three returned south and three rode eastward.

The three riding south also carried a puppy, Mussago's gift to his fellow nobleman. Daboreth thought he might well visit his neighbor — and his neighbor's granddaughter — again soon.

Donzalo, Copago and Guesare followed the highway that would carry them toward County Rosam. In Dordos's lands, it would meet with the road to King's Pass and then on to the river and Ros-town.

"Whoever told Mussago to pay more attention to his roads should tell him again," complained Sir Copago.

"Be thankful that we are on horseback," responded Guesare. "A wagon would find the going near impossible in places."

"Such as one filled with brimstone," Donzalo remarked.

"Aye. A train of pack-horses might be needed."

They had passed several such on the road, going in both directions. It seemed the preferred mode of transport.

"That's all well and good for merchants going through Doram Pass," said Donzalo, "but not so suited to our needs." They continued in silence. In places, there were small gullies across their path.

"Riders are coming," spoke Guesare. "Three, I believe." He undid the thong that secured his rifle in its tooled scabbard, presented to him by Habidros before they left Count Orgelo's keep. Much fine leather-work was done in Tod-ford.

Naturally, Habi had not wished to be outshone by his brother Galaro, who had gifted the rifle in the first place.

That the men were soldiers was evident as they approached. Their leader's close helmet kept them from readily making out his features.

"Hail, Sir Donzalo!" called the man. "Have you come to give me more fencing lessons?"

"Blen? When did you grow that beard, man?"

"When I came over the mountains. I've enough to do without taking time to shave. Sir Guesare, Sir Copago! Greetings to you as well.

"Will you come visit me in my camp? 'Tis not far."

He turned his horse and started away, clearly expecting them to follow. Donzalo looked at his companions and then at the two armored soldiers, and shrugged. "Why not?" said he, and followed the Sharshite knight.

It was, indeed, not far, only a short distance off the road. "Another league or so," said Blen, pointing eastward, "and you would have left Mussago's lands. The count told me you were coming."

"Then you are here as his guests?" asked Guesare.

"One might so say. Think of it as Count Mussago doing a favor for King Lareth. Incidentally," he said, turning to Donzalo, "the king no longer desires your life."

"That is — fortunate," replied the young Laman.

"Not so fortunate is that Radal still wishes you dead, for whatever reasons he may have. I'm not sure even Lareth knows what those are."

Guesare and Donzalo glanced at each other. They knew well what lay behind the sorcerer's hatred. Blen could not help notice but said nothing.

"Sharsh is concerned about the situation at your home, Donzalo," continued Sir Blen. "That is why we are here. Your brother grows more erratic and Lord Radal is somewhere, plotting something. We must be ready if things fall apart in Lama.

"Perhaps you might stay with us tonight and fill me in on what is happening in County Arvaram. We do not know if Orgelo intends to get involved but it wouldn't hurt to know how the wind blows there."

"It blows eastward, Blen, sending me home."

~ ~ ~

So, his father would remain at Mountain Keep and he must remain here, attending to the duties of governing.

Gawis put down the letter. All the king would tell his son was that he was keeping an eye on Lama and could not leave. The prince knew his father had been moving troops to the border; their orders had come across his own desk.

As had a report of his sister-in-law's pregnancy. There had been no official announcement from Modareth and Carrana, but it was not something that could be hidden from their staff there at Grenethas. Now, the pair and their entourage were headed back to the capital. Maybe his brother could be of some help to him here.

He sighed and walked to the westward-facing window. Gawis missed his wife. This fact surprised him. Not long ago, he would have been distracted from such thoughts by his circle of hangers-on, by wine, by the many women who were always willing to be with him. It was good that she and the girls were out of Celatas for a while, down on the coast where the sea breezes kept summer heat at bay.

But he hoped she would return soon. Maybe Mara and he could even come up with an announcement to rival that of his brother. Gawis smiled at the thought. Why not? They had already produced three daughters.

His brother — he had best prepare for his arrival. There was still need to protect him from assassins. Perhaps the Lady Carrana as well, now, as she and the unborn child might also be targets. He would speak to the seneschal about setting up a guard, as well as preparing their quarters.

What if it is a boy? he wondered. It would be to his advantage if an assassin were successful. No, he would not wish such a thing.

Summer was fading. The astrologers would say that it was already over, now that the Festival of Abundance had passed and the equinox approached. Would they be harvesting the grapes in Arolin now? Cooler weather had already reached there but had not penetrated to the heartland of Sharsh.

Arolin. It would be wise to move some troops about there so the Muram wouldn't think Sharsh had all its attention focused on Lama. Father would approve of that, wouldn't he?

Yes. Gawis turned from his view of Celatas and the River Chas and far beyond those, hidden from him, the sea, and sat to write the order.

~ ~ ~

Sir Blen had bidden goodbye to his guests and watched them ride into the dawn. He guessed it would take them near a week to reach the Weldar, as they were not hurrying nor would they have a change of horses. In his courier days, he could have made the journey in well less than half that time.

Then they intended to cross the Weldar south of Ros-town and ford the Abam somewhere upstream, traveling on to the keep of Sir Paren. He hoped they were not underestimating the dangers of their journey.

Of course, Bolos would receive word from his border guards that his brother had returned, even if he did skirt Castle Rosam on his way. Most probably, Orgelo had sent him a message as well, saying to expect Donzalo.

Ten days, perhaps, for the entire trip. Much could happen in ten days. Perhaps he would use that time to ride down to Todmouth himself and hear what news there might be.

He could see a pair of riders coming down the road. A man and a boy, it appeared, perhaps a knight or man at arms and his attendant, for they were on fine horses and he could discern a glint of armor. For a moment, Blen considered waiting there and speaking with them.

No, better he get on to other, more urgent errands. He turned back toward his encampment and let them pass.

~ ~ ~

His spies told him the boy was on the move. Radal considered sending his men, all his men, out to intercept him and be done with it. Too rash, perhaps — if those men failed and were scattered or destroyed, there might never be another chance.

Still, he was as unprotected as he was ever likely to be. Donzalo and his companions were reportedly headed back to County Rosam. Yes, he would chance it.

Not Radal himself. Not now. There were other schemes he must be ready to put into action and that were best done here. Soon, though, he would leave this broken tower where once had dwelt the wizard Sabatare.

He went down to the entry, where the tall oaken doors stood ajar, and called one of the attendants lounging in the overgrown courtyard. "I shall have a message for your sergeant shortly. Be ready to carry it to him."

~ ~ ~

Pol attempted to show that he was not in awe.

Until now, the largest city he had known was Oles. It was as nothing beside Celatas.

As he had throughout their journey, he rode only half a horse's length behind his prince, ready to act if need be. With the twenty sturdy troopers accompanying them, it seemed unlikely that such a need would arise. Still, Pol saw that as no reason to be slack in his duties.

Here, Modareth should be well guarded in his father's keep, the young knight's constant presence no longer required. He would miss the prince's company and his learned talk. He would miss the library at Grenethas. He had learned a great deal reading there.

But surely there were many books here in Celatas. They *made* books here. Pol smiled to himself. If Jobareth Nafal could have books printed, why not he?

The young knight had never really intended a military career. He had joined the army when his family had all been slain in the war against the Mura. That conflict ended before he had a chance to see action and, a couple of years later, Pol had found himself in Lama.

That, he felt, was one of the most fortunate events in his life. Had it not led to all that had happened in this past year, when he had risen from an ordinary soldier to a knight and the personal bodyguard of a prince? Had it not made him a friend of the Viscountess Fachalana? Had Pol any great belief in the gods he might have thanked them.

Prince Modareth motioned to him to move alongside. "My lord?" he asked.

"I just wanted to point out the King's Bridge," said the prince, gesturing toward the left of their route. Pol did not even try to hide his wonder this time.

"Do we cross it, sir?" He was perhaps a little apprehensive of such an action.

"No, my father's keep is to our right, above the city. We should see it soon — yes, there it is." It towered on the heights, as much a crown as the one the king wore on his head. The hills below it were dotted with the manicured villas of the wealthy and aristocratic.

Pol thought it looked rather similar to Keep Rosam, though obviously larger.

"Keep close to me, Pol," said Modareth, "and don't let yourself be rattled." The prince, being of a shy disposition, knew the hazards of entering an unfamiliar situation.

And Pol, although of a brasher sort, recognized and was grateful for his young patron's concern.

7

"Who is this Prince Modareth?" asked the guard, looking over their papers.

Fachalana was exasperated but Ansa spoke before her companion could say something rash. "He is the younger son of King Lareth, good sir."

"Humph. Why have I never heard of him?"

Fachalana had regained her composure. She spoke in the low gravelly voice she had adopted. "Surely you have heard of his great vineyards in Dor? Their fame is widely sung. The Prince Modareth has produced his marvelous vintages there for many years."

The man had heard of the wine of Dor and that it had a good reputation. He was therefor willing to believe the rest. Ansa was almost willing to believe it herself.

"Very well," he said, handing back their passports. "Count Dordos is a friend of Sharsh. You have proper diplomatic papers and need not pay the toll."

"Thank you, sir," replied the disguised noblewoman in her heartiest tones. "Would that the guards at our last two border crossings had felt the same. Saj, do give our friend a little tip for his courtesy." Ansa doled out a couple coppers. She suspected that the man got a cut of the tolls so it did not hurt to alleviate his loss and perhaps buy some good will. Ansa was a little surprised that Fachalana had also recognized this. The lady was learning the ways of the world.

"Sir," she asked, "have there been other fighting men through here of late?"

"You consider yourself a fighting man, lad?" he laughed. "Three fellows passed late yesterday. I think they were in a hurry to reach the river and make a crossing under cover of night." He lowered his voice, as if letting them in on a secret. "I recognized one as Count Borrago's old master of arms. He would sometimes tour the border crossings. From the other side, you know."

"Ah, what was his name?" said Fachalana. "Copago, wasn't it?"

"Aye, sir. Know you the man?"

"I have seen him at Keep Rosam." Which was quite the truth. "A solid man."

"That he is. The new count has treated him poorly." The man looked up at them. "Go you to visit Count Bolos?"

"That, good sir, I am not at liberty to say. A good day to you. Come, Saj." Fachalana rode through the gate, followed by her faithful esquire.

~ ~ ~

He had wasted his time, waiting here by the river, while Guesare and his companions had traveled through the hills. A tinker who had of late visited County Arvaram brought Perdos that information.

"I must say," the man told him, "I was glad to see the minstrel's brother head south. It is hard to compete with his band of traders."

"And the other brother remains at Tod-ford?"

"Aye. It is rumored that he will marry the count's niece. That may provide an occasion to make some sales." The peddler squinted at Perdos from beneath a well-worn turban. "Is there anything I might interest you in today, sir?"

The knight glanced at his wares. "Pots and pans? No, not today but perhaps some day soon."

As the man's cart disappeared up the road, Perdos readied his horse and gear. It was time to ride north, back toward County Rosam. Where else might they be headed?

Back to where it all began. That would be the place to finally take his vengeance.

~ ~ ~

Dovolo was baffled. They had waited on the road, west of the river, for the Rosam boy and his companions to ride into town. The plan was to waylay them among the warehouses and sheds that lined the road down to the ferry. It was dangerous to act so close to Ros-town but, at the same time, the men could fade into the crowds usually found at the river's edge.

But their intended victims had never appeared. At last he sent some men up the road to look for them. There was no sign.

"They musta crossed somewheres else, Sergeant," opined one of his ruffians.

Then they must not be headed for Ros-town at all, thought Dovolo. Where? Unfortunately, the man, though a capable enough leader, did not really know the area nor much about the Rosam family.

Another of his men spoke up. "Maybe they went to Paren's place, up the Abam."

There were murmurs of agreement to that.

"In other words," said Dovolo, "had we stayed in our encampment, they might have come riding right past us."

He hoped Lord Radal had a sense of humor.

~ ~ ~

"I like the colors, my brother."

Prince Gawis laughed. "They make my life simpler. I need not think about what I shall put on each morning!"

"I have that problem no longer," replied Modareth. "Carrana feels it her duty to choose my wardrobe."

The elder prince nodded. He was not at all surprised that his brother's wife would so take charge. Modi tended to be impractical and absent-minded.

Or the Modi he remembered, at any rate. His brother seemed no longer quite the man he remembered. More mature, more aware of the world around him — perhaps twice escaping assassination attempts had that effect on one.

"I understand the Princess Carrana is with child."

"Yes. We will make an official announcement shortly. I did not want to distract Father with the news." Though he attempted to say all this as soberly as possible, his brother could see he was delighted by the thought of becoming a father.

Again Gawis laughed. "Do not think that he is unaware of it!

43

Father would have received regular reports from your household. As did I," he added. Should I have told him that? wondered the prince.

"I must hire some spies of my own, I suppose," mused the younger man.

"Who is that fellow who follows you about? Is he the one who captured the assassin?" Sir Pol had accompanied his prince to Gawis's office and waited now outside the door.

"He is. Pol is his name and he is a bright lad if ever there were one. To be honest, Brother, I am not sure what to do with him now. Sir Pol is meant for better things than serving as my bodyguard, I am certain."

"Perhaps he could be one of those spies you say you need," suggested Gawis, meaning it mostly as jest.

Modareth thought it a most excellent idea.

~ ~ ~

The guard looked over their papers and then looked up at them. "Is the ambassador expecting you?"

"No, he is not," came the weary reply. "But you might inform Legate Nafal that I bear a message from the Lady Fachalana."

He considered this briefly. "Very well. Come on into the stables and rest while I send someone up." The pair dismounted and entered while a groom hurried up the stairs to find the legate.

Shortly, Jobareth himself came down. That he immediately saw through his life-long friend's disguise is no surprise. He said nothing of it in front of the soldiers and servants. "Sir Jan, welcome to our embassy. Come on up to my office and we shall discuss your message. Your attendant, too — what is your name, boy?"

"Saj, sir."

"Then come along, Saj. Take care of their horses and gear, will you?" he called to the group watching them. As soon as the trio passed out of their sight, they burst into laughter.

"Fachalana, it is good to see you," said Jobareth, embracing her. "You too, Ansa-Maresta-Posena-Saj!" He stepped back to look at the pair. "And what in the name of Jov are you up to?"

"We are but knights errant, seeking adventure," said Ansa, "and the welfare of our friends."

"Ah. Does that include me?"

"You know it does, Jobo," replied Lady Fachalana. "And Lomela and Donzalo and even Sir Blen."

"Well, come on up to my office and I shall have refreshments brought and you can tell me of your journey. And then we must decide what to do with you!"

Tell him of their journey they did, as well as their time in Sharsh. It was a long tale and a long journey and they were tired at the end.

"So then, we were approaching the river and saw a band of most vile ruffians," said Fachalana. "I did fear we might be attacked."

"As did I," said Ansa, "but they seemed to be hurrying off on some urgent errand. I led us down to a place where one can quietly hire a boat to cross the Weldar, if one knows the correct words."

"Being a spy has its advantages," observed Jobareth.

"And then we rode straight here," finished Fachalana, "Sir Jan and his esquire Saj."

"It will be impossible to keep your identities secret if you stay here at the embassy," said Jobareth. "And I should tell Lord Doufan about you."

"Don't tell your secretary. Neither we nor Sir Pol trust him," warned Ansa.

"I don't quite myself," replied the legate. "It will take a while for me to think of my young protege as the heroic Sir Pol!

"Well, I can quietly find you some quarters here for the night. If, in the morning, you feel you wish to continue to go incognito, I think I know just the place where you can stay."

~ ~ ~

"I have avenged you," said Sir Perdos, standing by the two graves near the burnt-out inn, "as best I can." Would that he could have destroyed every man who had been part of this. Still, slaying their leader had provided a great deal of satisfaction. The rest would no doubt grace one gallows or another someday.

He looked toward the ruins, the blackened stones of the chimney still standing as a sort of monument to what had been. Perhaps the best he could do for the innkeeper and his wife now would be to rebuild what they had once created.

"Now, my own vengeance," said he. "Then shall I return." Perdos mounted and rode north.

8

So, Sir Copago had returned and was now his uncle's master of arms. Bolos deemed this suspicious. There had been many strange comings and goings lately.

Armed bodies of masterless men moving about. Two strange fighting men who had shown up at the Sharshite embassy and then disappeared again.

And his brother Donzalo. Why had he gone to Uncle Paren's rather than coming first here? He was far too friendly with Copago.

No, they would not be plotting against him. Nor would his uncle be party to any disloyalty.

There were rumors of Sharshite troops across the Weldar, on the lands of Count Dordos. Orgelo, too, seemed to prepare for some sort of action and had sent his son out, ostensibly to deal with outlaws. Might there be more to that?

He turned to his ever faithful sergeant, Jak. He was the one man in the world Bolos trusted completely. He must find a proper gift for the fellow's upcoming wedding.

For a moment, the count's gloom was dispelled. Who would have thought this middle-aged soldier, a bachelor all his life, would find love now? Somehow, it seemed fitting that the most trusted servants of his wife and himself should wed.

Perhaps it would make up in some way for the love that had never existed between Bolos and the Princess Lomela.

"Jak," said he, "have you seen Sir Corgos today?"

"He is inspecting the walls this morning, my lord."

A good man, Corgos. He was thankful to his uncle for graciously allowing the knight to change to his service. Perhaps letting Paren have Sir Copago was only fair.

He would not complain about it, but Count Bolos still did not like it.

"Let us ride out ourselves. I could use some air." It could help clear his head. Better than sitting here in his chambers with the temptation of wine close at hand. He should stop drinking, Bolos told himself. He had done it before.

Before his father died, and his daughter. Before threats had seemed to beset him on every side.

"I'll bring the horses around, sir," said Sir Jak.

~ ~ ~

"The word is that Donni is at his uncle Paren's and both will soon come here."

"Is Sir Copago there as well?" asked Ansa. "We were surprised to have news that he was riding before us on our journey, having heard that he was in the service of Count Orgelo."

"He left that service to become Paren's master of arms," Jobareth replied. "I know not why. I do know that Donzalo's former shadow, Habidros, took his place there in County Arvaram."

"I liked Habidros," said Ansa.

"Do you like every man you meet?" Fachalana asked. Ansa had never shown this side of herself when she was an actress back in Celatas.

Not your father, Ansa said to herself. "What was not to like about Sir Habidros? Handsome, bold, and very tall. Not unlike Donzalo."

But not Donzalo. That thought came to both women.

"Do you intend to continue your masquerade, my ladies? Even here, that may prove difficult." Jobareth had installed them in the modest house the Sharshite embassy rented in Ros-town. He had also informed the ambassador, Lord Doufan, of their presence.

Both were puzzled by the sudden appearance of the pair. "Use your own judgment, my boy," Doufan had told him, "but do keep me informed." That was not out of character for the diplomat.

"If we reveal our identities, the knowledge of it will be everywhere within a week. Even Sharsh."

Jobareth suspected that Doufan had already sent a message to King Lareth with just that information. He would have, were he in the same position. How the king might act, he had no idea.

"Then you will remain Jan and Saj? If you don't leave the house much you might get away with it." The old butler who kept this house for him would be discreet, even if he noticed anything odd about the guests.

"But that itself would be suspicious," Ansa pointed out, "and there wouldn't be much point in coming here if we do not intend to do anything, would there?"

"I am the problem," stated Fachalana. "Ansa could mask herself in many ways but I know that I do stand out with my height and coloring."

"Then Sir Jan remains your best disguise," replied her companion. "There is no point in throwing away an identity you have already established. And," she went on, "it will allow you to ride freely about the countryside."

"Unless Bolos or some zealous fellow who serves him wonders about this stranger and has him taken in for questioning," said Jobareth. "I think I shall ask Lord Doufan if I can issue you diplomatic credentials. If you seem attached to the embassy, there will be fewer questions.

"Enough now, of this. I shall call to have food and chilled wine brought up, and we shall enjoy this evening as old friends rather than conspirators."

"I would enjoy that, Jobo," said Lady Fachalana. "But first I ask one more thing of you: do not let Lomela know we are here."

Jobareth Nafal nodded his assent and rang for the butler.

~ ~ ~

No harm, one way or the other, thought Lord Radal. He had not ended Donzalo Rosam's life but neither had he lost any men. Things could move forward according to his plans.

It would have been good, though, to have brought it all to a close. The longer the young Laman lived, the more he might pose a threat to the future of Fachalana. Radal could not shake his conviction that their destinies were entwined.

It was enough that Donzalo's involvement had led to the death of one daughter, the daughter he had not known he had. For that alone did he hate him enough to wish his death. He would not chance the fate of the other.

He still had spies on the other side of the mountains and they reported that his daughter had disappeared from Sharsh. Radal suspected that she had reentered Lama. Distance meant little to his sorcery but mattered quite a lot in the physical world.

And his spy at the Sharshite embassy in County Rosam had heard that two strangers had appeared in the night, to closet with Legate Nafal and disappear again the next morning. Could the pair have been Fachalana and her friend, Maresta?

He could only tell the man to keep watch. Fortunately, his reports could come to the sorcerer more quickly than those of his other minions. Radal felt a certain distaste for the fellow; he sensed that he had no center to him, no feelings for anyone but himself and his own appetites. Benawis was not a man to trust.

On the other hand, he was rather pleased with how well the newly-made sergeant of his small company had performed. The man had been, of course, rightly fearful of Radal after Donzalo slipped by them. It was good to have ones followers feel a little fear. But he had done well in handling the situation and seemed to have a head on his shoulders. Dovolo would do.

Soon he might have the chance to prove himself further.

~ ~ ~

Sir Paren had chosen to take no chances on the road, remembering the events of the previous year, and had brought a number of doughty men at arms along with him, with Donzalo riding safely in their midst.

Also among them was Dame Tiana. The woman had refused a wagon, saying it would slow them, and rode as well. Paren hoped that was wise and chose the gentlest horse in his stables for her.

"Now, do you think we should expect your husband to be waiting at the outer gate for us?" he asked her as they neared Castle Rosam.

"He had better be," replied Tiana. "Or even better, meet us on the road."

"Then perhaps this approaching cloud of dust is he," said the knight.

Tiana smiled. She knew her Corgos.

The master of arms reined his steed in as he reached them. "I have been watching for you from the walls. Welcome to your new home, Wife!" He bowed toward the reeve. "Greetings, Sir Paren, and my thanks to you. My thanks for many things! Donzalo, my boy! Greetings to you as well."

Such exuberance was unusual for the man, but all there understood it.

Through the three gates of Keep Rosam they passed, between the great oaken doors of the outer wall, under the iron portcullis of the second, and finally beneath the arch in the thick inner walls, with its double gates. Into the broad courtyard they rode, its stone tower rising above them.

For Donzalo, this was a homecoming. Dame Tiana, however, had never seen so grand a place as her new abode. "Will we live there?" she asked her husband, looking toward the tower.

"No, wife of mine. We will have more comfortable apartments over, um, there," he said, pointing to a spot somewhere to the right of the stables. Sir Corgos had actually been residing in the tower, in Count Borrago's old quarters, and had paid little attention to the furnishing of his new rooms. "Ah, and there is the count. I must present you."

Bolos and his wife, the Lady Lomela, stood at the doorway of the Great Hall. He looks alert today, thought Corgos. Thank Kamat for that.

The count welcomed the knight's wife gravely and soberly. Quite literally soberly, he was glad to see. Then Lomela embraced her and led her off to wherever women went.

By then, Bolos was shaking the hands of his uncle and brother. They were welcome enough in Keep Rosam, it seemed and would find their ways here. It was best he got back to his own duties.

Well, first, he should look in on Tiana and make sure she had found her way to their new apartment. Corgos was not absolutely sure where that was, right then, but knew he would soon get used to going there. It had been a long time since Corgos had been part of a family, near twenty years as soldier and roving mercenary, as a man without a home.

This would be his home now that his wife — and, soon enough, a third — was here.

~ ~ ~

The ferry crossing lay well outside County Arvaram, but he who ruled here as count had readily granted Sorsen permission to cross his lands. What had happened at this little village had much to do with that.

He and Sir Habidros surveyed what remained of the burnt inn. "It does not seem the work of ordinary bandits," stated Sir Sorsen.

"No, my lord," replied Habidros. "I would guess a military company of some sort." He had seen too many such ruins as a mercenary and had taken part in a few such actions himself.

"Nothing to be learned here," said Sorsen, and turned his horse toward the river.

There they found the cook Hendel at his stall and heard much the same story from him that he had told Perdos a few weeks earlier. At the name of Sojel, the two leaders looked at each other knowingly.

"So, Sir Perdos has already brought our culprit to justice," spoke Habidros.

"Perdos, my lords? He was here and told me the innkeeper and his wife had been his friends. He seemed greatly moved by their deaths." Hendel had recognized the knight from his days at Castle Rosam, but had felt it best not to let Perdos know this. Both men had pasts of which they would rather not speak. "It is good that he took vengeance for them."

"Only on their leader. The company may still be about somewhere," observed Sir Sorsen. "What say you, Sir Habidros? Shall we go look for sign of them?"

"North or south?" asked the Cuddonian.

"North," replied Sorsen. "If these men rode with Sojel then they were in the pay of Lord Radal. They might be seeking our friend Donzalo."

"Then let us ride, sir! But if there be trouble, remember to let my pistoleers protect your hussars from danger. It would not do to let any of them be harmed unnecessarily."

"Ha, my lancers would overwhelm them before your men got off their first shot!"

The two rode north along the Great Road, their column behind them, and each hoping for the chance to prove the other wrong.

9

"There is someone at our door."

Fachalana came to the window and stuck her head out alongside Ansa's. "I don't think I know him," she said. But the gentleman *did* look familiar, didn't he?

The butler was opening the door to him. The old fellow seemed to know the man, whoever he was.

"We had best don our man-clothes," said Ansa.

"And slip out the back?" Fachalana asked.

"Maybe."

"No need to hide yourselves, my ladies," came a voice from the foot of the stairs. "I am quite harmless."

In sudden recognition, Fachalana stated, "That is Lord Doufan."

"And he has let the butler in on our secret," replied Ansa. There was both resignation and a certain peevishness to her voice.

"Did you really think he hadn't noticed by now? You put far too much trust in the efficacy of your disguises, my friend!"

True, thought Ansa. Even when she had first come to Lama, Donzalo had surmised something of her actual identity.

"We shall be right down, sir," Fachalana called. To Ansa she whispered, "I think we should dress as Jan and Saj anyway. Best we stay in character."

"It will confuse the butler," the Anian replied.

Doufan was dressed as he did when he prowled Ros-town incognito, looking more like an old soldier in worn buff-coat and breeches, a longsword dangling at his side. The aged servant held a wide-brimmed hat the ambassador had doffed.

"Ah, Sir Jan," said Lord Doufan as the pair descended. "And this must be your esquire Saj. I give you greetings, gentlemen."

Ansa noted the slight smile playing about the old butler's mouth. Well, Jobareth had said to trust in the man's discretion.

"Lord Doufan," Fachalana replied, giving the man a small and courteous bow. "What might we do for you this fine day?" She used her masculine voice. Fachalana had practiced it quite a lot now and thought she did it well.

"You might dine with me, if you do not mind going out in public. We might, so to speak, put your identities to test in a tavern. But mostly," he continued, "I came to bring you these." Doufan handed an apparently official document to each woman.

"So we are now diplomats?" asked Ansa.

"Indeed. Or, more properly, soldiers attached to the embassy. That should get you through most difficulties you might encounter." He then spoke more lowly, more seriously. "I know not why you are here and perhaps I should not be aiding you. Will you come with me and explain yourselves over ale and a meal? I have a craving for fowl today. They serve it fried here, you know."

"They seem to serve everything fried in Lama," responded Lady Fachalana. "We shall gladly share some chicken with you."

There was a tavern not far away and near the river. Lord Doufan had built a personal knowledge of all such establishments in Rostown. The rich, heavy scent of fried fish and fowl hung in the air as they entered. Fachalana was not sure whether it enticed or revolted her, but she allowed Doufan to order fried fowl for both her and himself.

Ansa, however, who knew more of Laman cuisine, asked for catfish. Lord Doufan nodded approvingly of her taste.

As did Fachalana, after she picked a bit of it off her friend's plate. She liked it far better than the chicken on her own. Chickens should be roasted only, she decided, or made into soup.

A passing whore eyed her and then squinted at Ansa. That she had seen through their guises was Fachalana's immediate thought. Then she realized that the woman was only wondering if the 'boy' was too young. Doufan waved her away from their table, its dark wood saturated with the grease of thousands of meals, and began to speak in a low voice.

"You are concerned about your father's plans here, are you not, Jan?" Doufan was every bit as good an actor as these two and not one to break character — his or anyone else's. "Especially as they concern your friends."

Fachalana nodded. Then she realized something and whispered, "How shall we name you here, sir?"

The ambassador laughed. "Around here they have taken to calling me Old Dog. Ask not why for I am not sure! But 'tis as good a name as any."

Neither woman could quite see herself addressing the ambassador so. Doufan, recognizing this, added, "The young ladies tend to name me Grandfather. Why not use that?

"But, back to our subject. Why do you think you can be of any use here?" He looked at Ansa. "You, as a well-trained spy, might be of some assistance. Yes, I know much of your past. But you?" Doufan looked intently at Fachalana. "Excellence with a sword is all well and good but what else have you to offer?"

The two women looked at each other. "It is up to you," Ansa said to her friend. "Tell him if you will."

Lady Fachalana hesitated. Not even the king was aware of her secret, nor were most of her friends. She thought Donzalo might have an inkling, having known her sister.

Why should she speak of it to this courtier?

"I — share in my father's gifts, sir."

"Ah." The ambassador said no more for quite a long while. "He has trained you in their use?" he asked at last.

"Yes." She sighed deeply — it seemed almost a sob — and went on. "Right now, I hide from my father and fear to use what I have learned lest he find me."

"Do you fear you might be used as a weapon against us?"

"If he were able to read my secrets, yes." This was indeed Fachalana's greatest fear.

"But you might read his as well. Is this not so?"

"Yes. I suppose that is true."

The group sat in silence again. Ansa drank of her ale and then spoke. "I think this should be the end of our luncheon, Grandfather Dog. We all have much to think upon now."

"That we do," agreed Lord Doufan.

~ ~ ~

"How could the Anian officers live in such a hole?" Jobareth Nafal looked about Donzalo's quarters with unconcealed distaste.

"That baffled me too," said Donzalo, "until I realized there was no floor above this level in those days. See up there? Those are the frames where skylights once opened this room to the air.

"Anians like to see the sky. I suspect that they actually slept out of doors as much as possible."

"Leave it to you to come up with a sensible explanation," replied the diplomat. "You haven't much here. Will your books remain at your uncle's?"

"Yes, and most of my other belongings. If you wish to read from my library, you must visit Sir Paren's keep."

"It might be worth the ride. Three days, isn't it? I've never been up that way."

"If I settle in there, I do expect you to visit, Legate. Bolos has named me the official heir so I suppose it is where I should be." Donzalo sounded less than enthusiastic about the idea. "Now, there is something you should see.

"This is a thing I would not show Sir Corgos. The man is too loyal to his duties to be trusted with such a secret." The young knight went to a spot on the side wall, close to the stone walls of the castle itself that bounded the far end of the chamber. There he opened the hidden panel that revealed a secret passage.

The Sharshite eyed the opening and then his friend. "Now I understand why you chose these quarters."

"I know not if I shall long remain here and I wish you to be able to reach the Lady Lomela, should it become necessary. So I trust you and no other, Jobareth Nafal, with this." He started down the steep stairway hewn into the rock. "Come along."

"We should have one of these at the embassy," joked Jobareth, following his friend down a sloping tunnel.

"Oh, um, the rumor is that Blen had one put in while you were gone."

"Indeed? I must ask him about this when he returns!"

They entered the cave at the end of the passage.

"We are on the cliffs?" asked Nafal. Donzalo nodded and pointed toward the narrow opening in the rock. The legate peered through this doorway to the outside world.

"There is a ledge one can follow. Or so Copago claims; I have not attempted it."

"I do not blame you. And," continued Jobareth, "I hope you never need to."

~ ~ ~

It was unusual for Count Mussago to leave his keep in the hills. He was not young, and somewhat stout, nor had he ever been a man of action.

His eldest son accompanied him. He looked as much a farmer fresh from the fields as did his father. Perhaps he was.

"We received your news of Sorsen," said the count. "Do you intend to act?"

"My lord, I know not his plans. It would be rash to commit Sharsh at this time." Blen knew only that Orgelo's heir had led a company of men out of County Arvaram and was riding north on the Great Road. He claimed to do no more than search for outlaws.

"None need know Sharsh is involved if you ride under my colors. I intend to send a few men under the command of my boy here," he said, placing his gloved hand on the middle-aged man's shoulder, "to make an official visit to County Rosam. There is no reason your company could not ride along."

Blen nodded slowly. He must make a decision. Should he take his men across the river? "Very well, my lord. I must send messages to Sharsh about the action I have chosen."

"Of course." Mussago turned to his son.

"Let Sir Blen command," he told him, "and keep out of the way."

~ ~ ~

Could all Lama soon be thrown into conflict? Oder and his superiors were not unduly concerned about Sharsh's actions — they knew there were enough tensions among the counts to bring war to the entire region, with or without outside involvement.

The Anian spy had sent a complete report along as soon as he reached one of their stations in western Lama. It was high in the mountains, that station, a little cottage in the wild lands where no one ruled. A courier had left immediately but it would take weeks for his information to reach any maker of decisions.

Which meant he might need to make the decisions.

And why not? Oder might have been a general, had he chosen. But he preferred this life and it was where his natural talents lay. Moreover, he suspected that most of the battles of the Anian Empire in the years to come would be losing ones.

Lamans hated Anians. This was a given. None would openly ally themselves with the Empire. Yet, behind the scenes, who might say? There were those who loved neither Sharsh nor An Corade, the two great players in the valley of the Weldar. There were those desired only peace and stability and would welcome the continued Anian presence in Morparas, gateway to Lama.

If the Ani ever lost that city, their power in the west would be at an end. It could not be regained. How long before the Siphic territories would follow?

He could go there. Although Morparas was officially a free city under Anian protection, there was an imperial garrison stationed there. But couriers already rode to warn them of trouble. Oder would not be of much use.

No, he would head into the center of things here in Lama, County Rosam. His old comrade and protege Guesare would be there. Most likely, so would his sister and her sorcerous friend. Even if his presence there proved of no aid to the empire, he could see to Ansa's safety.

To Keep Rosam, then, where much of this current trouble had its beginning. Where better for it to end?

10

Guesare had felt it best to leave Sir Paren's party before they entered the Rosam fortress. Bolos might or might not have tolerated his presence but he would not like it. That could color his relationship with his brother.

So another must guard Donzalo for a while. He should be safe enough in the keep, under the watchful eye of Sir Corgos, now that the king of Sharsh no longer sought his life. Only the sorcerer Radal, driven by his madness, pursued the boy.

Guesare still hated that man, as he had a year and a half earlier when he had first attempted to take Donzalo's life. And nearly succeeded in taking his own, as well. He hoped, when the time came, he would be the one to run a blade through Lord Radal. Though an arrow or even a bullet would give great satisfaction. He should practice more with that new rifle of his.

He had considered visiting Jobareth down at the embassy. But for what purpose? Donzalo would no doubt tell the diplomat that Guesare was in the area. Better to just stay in town a while, play the wandering minstrel for tips and meals, watch and wait. Things would happen, in their time.

From his seat in a small tavern, the sort of clean and rather wholesome place he preferred — to the surprise of many — he saw a trio in the street, an older man and two slender young soldiers. The one, indeed, no more than a boy. What was so familiar about them?

As they passed, he knew. Guesare laughed long and loudly and no one there knew why.

~ ~ ~

The river could be dammed up here, thought Copago, and a waterwheel placed right over there.

"What are you mulling over now, my husband?" asked the woman by his side.

"Nothing of importance, my dear." Felled trees came down the Abam. A way for them to pass the dam would have to be provided. Timber provided much of the income of Sir Paren's estate.

King ran ahead of them, barking at one of the dark fox squirrels that were plentiful here where farmland met forest.

Janona had greatly missed the knight while he spent his season in the service of Orgelo. She had expected, eventually, to be called to join him in Country Arvaram. To have him return and abide here at this rural keep was far better. Such a life was suited to Sir Copago.

It suited her, too, and their little daughter and, for that matter, King. Janona had grown up a country girl.

Copago put his arm around her as they strolled along the banks of the wild Abam.

~ ~ ~

Guesare had followed the girls and the man who could only be Lord Doufan back to their house. They knew he was following them, of course, but neither they nor he acknowledged it.

Doufan left them at the door and continued down the unpaved street. After a moment's hesitation, the minstrel decided to follow. The ambassador stopped before a livery stable and beckoned toward his shadow.

"Is there aught you need to know before I ride, sir?" he asked when Guesare reached his side. The man's expression was bland, pleasant, and quite unreadable.

"I was but on a voyage of discovery, my lord, so to speak."

"Call me not lord here. I am a simple old soldier to these people."

Guesare nodded. "I did not know my friends had returned."

"Sir Jan and his esquire? They are attached to the Sharshite embassy." There was an unmistakable twinkle in Lord Doufan's eye. "You should perhaps visit them while they are in town. Or inquire of them at the embassy."

An invitation. "Maybe so, sir. I did mean to call on the legate one of these days."

"I've no doubt he would welcome you. However," the older man advised, "you might do well to call first upon the ambassador."

Doufan said no more but turned and entered the stable.

THE HAND OF THE SORCERER

~ ~ ~

Some days were good for Bolos. On others, beset by fear and suspicion, he would fall. After, he hated himself for his weakness, wondering if there were any point in trying to be a better man.

There were many better men around him. Bolos felt, sometimes, like a boy in a room full of men. But he would have to depend on those men.

Rumors spoke of troops massing, or already on the move, all over Lama. Beyond, as well — Sharsh had moved men to its borders and the Coradeans and Ani were sure to follow that lead.

He must send word to all his captains, telling them to be watchful. Maybe he should ask his uncle for some of his troops, or conscript more young men of the countryside into his service.

That he could trust Sir Corgos to take care of any necessary actions here at the castle, he knew. Corgos was one of those better men. He seemed a happier man, too, now that his wife was here. The count found himself liking Dame Tiana, with her sharp, humorous observations. The Lady Lomela, it seemed, wasn't always sure what to make of Keep Rosam's newest resident.

Lomela. They had grow distant again, hadn't they? She spent more time with his brother, or that diplomat Nafal, than with him. For a moment, Bolos believed that maybe he hated his brother.

He should not be suspicious of Donzalo. The boy had never done him harm. Not intentionally.

Bolos sipped from his cup of barley-brew. It had grown lukewarm.

Donzalo was a knight now, a fighting man and a good one, by all reports. He should have a post if trouble came. No sense in wasting him up at their uncle's estate.

But either way, he would not mind having him out of the keep again.

~ ~ ~

There was talk of war on the streets of Celatas. It was inaccurate, mostly, and some of it might have been deemed reckless. The authorities attempted to keep that to a minimum.

People must be allowed to speak their minds. It makes them think that they are free. Lord Doufan had said that; Pol had paid close attention to things the experienced statesman might say as they had journeyed from Sharsh to County Rosam. It had been a long trip and there had been much idle time for listening.

He was right, thought Pol. Let them talk. Listen to them as if you were interested in their point of view and then do whatever you feel is best.

Young Sir Pol had spent much time lately exploring the capital city. It intrigued him, the shops, the temples, the great banking houses, and, most of all, the theaters, just now beginning to open for the new season. He had found the shuttered establishment of Lady Fachalana. There would be no actors on its stage this year.

Rumors abounded as to her whereabouts, as well as those of her father. Most were wildly mistaken.

Prince Modareth had asked him to do this, to wander Celatas and learn its ways, and then tell him of what he had learned. The prince himself had become retiring since his return to the capital and spent much time in his well-guarded apartments.

But there were visitors to those rooms. Princess Carrana made certain of that and she also made certain that Pol could be there to meet them. The Arolinian shopkeeper's son-turned-knight now knew many of the most important and powerful people in Sharsh. He had even been introduced to Jobareth Nafal's father, a wealthy dealer in wines, but made no mention of knowing his son. After all, he had been only an ordinary soldier in his service — why bring that up?

Tonight, he was to meet the crown prince. His wife, the Princess Mara, had returned days before from the seashore with their children, and Gawis was hosting a party to mark the occasion. Pol had glimpsed the princess once in the halls of King's Keep, a slender, dark woman, who, according to gossip, was as shy as his own master.

He supposed Carrana would also keep introducing him to young women. That was all well and good but Pol had no time for such right now. There were so many things he wanted to do here, so many directions he wished to travel.

For Pol, all things had now become possible.

11

It was the Fay. Radal had become certain of this. They were giving their aid to his daughter, probably without her even realizing it.

The sorcerer did not entirely disapprove of this. Fachalana needed stability right now as she wrestled with her growing power. They had helped to keep her from straying down those dark paths to madness.

But it served to hinder his own attempts to communicate, as they hid her from him, gave her some safe haven he could not find and enter.

Now he knew who his opponents were and he knew also how to defeat them. Fairie was not his equal. The People of the Air had never been given such power.

They would frustrate him no longer.

Lord Radal climbed to the top floor of the crumbling tower he had appropriated as his base. Here, he kept the ebony cask containing the one object of power he had been able to bring with him from Mountain Keep. He would need it.

And he would need all his strength. Radal would be attempting great magics.

~ ~ ~

"Lord Doufan has been expecting you."

Guesare followed the scribe down the hall. The man seemed familiar. As they paused at the door, he asked, "Do I know you sir?"

The man turned and answered with a smile. "We met years ago in Lanlaz, Sir Guesare. I believe you sat in on one of my classes. I believe you also never paid your tuition."

"Oh, the university. How came you to be Doufan's secretary? If the question be not too personal."

"It is not. I decided to see the world and attached myself to the best man I could find."

"That simple?"

"Indeed yes, sir. That simple. Lord Doufan wishes to speak privately to you so I shall remain here."

That simple and not that simple, thought the scribe as he stood in the hall. He would not have met Doufan if the diplomat had not visited Lorj. He had been intrigued by the man and, chances were, would never leave him. It was a better and more interesting life than teaching dolts the declension of Muram nouns, anyway.

The ambassador got directly to the point, after waving Guesare into a chair. He took one beside him, rather than placing his oversize desk between them.

"Did you know that Lady Fachalana has sorcerous powers?"

"Yes, my lord. I have known for some time of her gifts." Thanks to the Prince of the Fay and his people.

"One might ask whether the lady shares her father's gift or his curse. I only learned when we ate together yesterday." Doufan paused for a moment. "I was almost certain that you knew or I would not have said anything to you of it.

"Your mother has powers, has she not?"

This man knows too many things, thought Guesare. "She does, sir. As do I, in small part." He might as well admit to that. "Do you know the story of Donzalo's time with us in the Cuddon?"

"I have heard rumors. Would you give me the tale?"

And so the minstrel did what perhaps he did best, tell a story. It was the story of Donzalo and Jola, half-sister to Fachalana, and their love. It was a story of sorcery and of loss.

When the tale ended, Doufan sat a while, staring into the cup he held. "So, not only Donzalo lost someone when Jola was slain, but also Radal," he said at last.

"We believe this is why he so hates Donzalo."

"Yet he brought it on himself by pursuing the boy. And no doubt hates himself equally."

Guesare deemed that quite likely. "It has driven him to madness."

"That is an occupational hazard with wizards, is it not?" asked the diplomat, not expecting an answer. "It must be watched for in Fachalana."

"Perhaps, as did Jola, she should dream a while in Fairie," said the Cuddonian. He would speak of that to Donzalo sometime.

Donzalo should learn that Jola's sister shared in her abilities. That thought led him to another. "Do you think Jobareth should know of all this?"

"I would allow Lady Fachalana to inform her friend in her own time. Unless, of course, circumstances require it.

"For now, I do hope you visit them there in town, Sir Guesare. Move into our house if you wish. Someone really should keep an eye on that pair!"

~ ~ ~

There would be no point in taking the main road directly to Ros-town, passing through Count Dordos's domain. There were already Sharshite troops secretly there anyway, in wait, and Blen would not wish to compromise them by riding boldly through.

No, he and the men of Count Mussago would angle south of east and hope to meet Sorsen along the Great Road. The distance was nearly the same from here.

Two-score of his troopers rode with him and near another score of Mussago's men. Sir Blen knew that the count could put a far larger force in the field if need be but wisely would not commit troops at this time. They were investigating, not going to war — he hoped.

Mussago's son — who was named also Mussago — rode beside him. He was a taciturn fellow, lean where his father was fat, and darkened by the sun. "This road now will lead directly to the Weldar," he said, after a day spent following winding dusty trails. It looked a fair road.

"Where does it end in relation to Ros-town?" asked the Sharshite knight. His courier duties had never taken him into these lands.

The man pondered the question before drawling, "Maybe four or five leagues south. Maybe more."

That was closer than Blen might have wished but there was no more time to waste. "That would be in County Rosam, wouldn't it? There is a ferry there?"

Mussago the Younger nodded. "There is a ferry but the crossing lies just below the Rosam border. We won't have to cross Dordos's borders, either. That's what you wanted, isn't it?"

"Indeed it is. Thank you, sir." It would be more than five leagues if the crossing was below County Rosam. Blen suspected that the ferry was not large and would require several trips to transport all his men.

Even the one at Ros-town would probably take three.

"Let's ride, men," he called. "If we want to beat Sir Sorsen we need to move!"

Ride they did, through sunbaked hills of grass and scrub that gradually grew greener. In time, fields of corn and of beans lay on either side of their way, and they crossed small streams. The great River Weldar lay ahead.

~ ~ ~

Now, the burgess of Oles were voicing their concern.

Madin sat patiently while his master scrutinized the letter, brow furrowed, and then ran his hand through his lank hair. Count Bolos's hair was thinning, wasn't it?

The man would get his thoughts together soon and dictate something. It would be up to Madin to better order those thoughts on paper and present the count with a reply he might sign. At least he was remaining sober most of these days.

"They don't like what's happening, up in Oles," muttered Bolos, to no one in particular. "But they worry only about trade being disrupted.

"They would welcome the Anians back, I think, if they thought it good for business."

Perceptive, thought Madin. The count was not the fool some thought him.

"I might myself, rather than let Sharsh and the Coradeans divvy up our land. What good was it to marry the daughter of King Lareth if he is going to plot against me?" He looked to his secretary. "Pardon me, Madin. I speak unwisely.

"Let us compose a fitting reply to Oles, letting them know that all

68

is under control here in County Rosam and denying all rumors. And perhaps asking them if they would commit to coming to our aid, if necessary."

~ ~ ~

It was not the butler who opened the door to Jobareth but the minstrel Guesare. Doufan had told him that the man might take up residence in their house.

"The young, um, gentlemen are upstairs, Legate. I sent the old man out to fetch some of your wine."

"I hope you have not been doing that too frequently," laughed Nafal. "I have little left of what I brought from Sharsh.

"So the ladies are maintaining their charade?"

"They are professionals," replied Guesare with complete serious- ness. "They would not break character." He looked to the stairs. "Here come Jan and Saj now."

"You may call us by our own names tonight," said Fachalana as she came forward and embraced her friend. "We may dress the part of men but we shall not play them now."

"And lovely women you are, even so clad," replied the diplomat.

"Indeed, were I the sort to marry a woman, Ansa would be my first choice," declared Guesare.

"Only because I remind you of my brother," the Anian dryly replied.

The door creaked behind them as the old butler entered with a covered pitcher. "It's not your best stuff, sir," said he to Jobareth, with a smile, "but then, it's not your worst either. Shall I leave it?"

"Yes, please. I think we shall sit out on the porch on this warm evening."

"I'll bring some candles, sir." The man disappeared into his pantry.

"Things are slowing down in Ros-town," observed Guesare as they sat watching the stars slide down toward the Weldar. "There is another one of those Laman feast days coming, isn't there?"

69

"Autumn Feast," replied Jobareth, "when they mark the equinox. It is primarily a religious occasion here."

"But there are celebrations, too," Ansa said. "Dancing will most surely occur."

"Oh, the Lamans will dance anytime," observed Jobareth Nafal, "and then turn around and follow it with a solemn day of fasting."

"What good is a fast without also a feast?" asked Guesare. "Otherwise it is but self-denial for its own sake."

"Now you sound like our friend Grippo. Is the boy still up at Sir Paren's keep?" he asked Guesare.

"He is, and likely to remain now his brother has taken up residence," replied the minstrel.

"Too bad. He is wasted there."

Fachalana had been following this exchange with interest. She did not think she had ever fasted in her life. "What is the purpose of fasting? It seems an odd practice."

"Our abstinences should make us better appreciate our pleasures and help us recognize those things that are important to our lives." Ansa had spoken very quietly but very clearly.

Guesare nodded approvingly. "Now I wish to marry you all the more, my dear."

Fachalana laughed gaily. "You can add our Guesare to your list, right behind Blen and Pol." Then, she suddenly stiffened.

"No." Her long fingers were whitening where they gripped the arms of her chair.

"What is it, Lana?" exclaimed Ansa, going immediately to her side.

"It is — my father!"

And with that, the Lady Fachalana fell into a faint.

12

In Celatas, a man in a long gray tunic felt the disturbance. Lord Radal, he knew at once, and shuddered. He was no match for that man, perhaps the mightiest mage alive. "Wine," he called to the bar maid. Enough would dull his mind to what was happening in the other realms.

His own master would sense this too, he knew. There would be no contact between them this night.

And no need. Their plan was already laid and action ready to be taken.

The wizard could not help but think Radal had been somehow involved in stopping their first attempt at assassination. Had it not been his own daughter who interfered? How he could have known of it was, and would most likely remain, a mystery.

Nothing would stop them this time, not even that boy of a body-guard.

He drank deeply of the cheap red vintage and called for more.

~ ~ ~

Guesare carried the limp form of Fachalana into the house and laid her upon a couch.

"I do not understand," said Jobareth Nafal. "What has Lord Radal to do with this?"

The minstrel turned to him. "Our Fachalana has inherited the powers of her father. He seeks to link her mind to his."

"She has long been able to block him," said Ansa, looking up from where she knelt by her friend's side. "She has struggled with her father many times and won.

"I do not know what has changed."

Fachalana. Speak to me.

No, Father. She looked for a way to escape. Where was her refuge, her silver land?

She felt it was near but she could not see it.

Your friends can not help you.

Friends? What friends? Someone had been aiding her, hadn't they? Fachalana realized of a sudden. *Help me!* she cried.

We can not. Your father has found us out. He has blocked our way. The voices seemed far off.

You must do it yourself. She heard no more.

A door, she thought. All I need is a door and my sanctuary will lie on the other side. The door is — there.

It was. She stepped through.

I can follow you now, my daughter. Do not run from me. There was hurt in his voice. Her father loved her, she knew, but she could not let him in. It was too dangerous.

On the silver plain she stood, the plain where she had first glimpsed Donzalo. But Radal had been there as well, that time. It was true that he could enter here. There were no longer any wards against him.

If she could only reach that far, gleaming building, find safety behind its tall silver doors. Fachalana knew she would be safe there. *Come,* said a voice, a beautiful golden woman's voice, *and I shall keep thee safe.*

Who are you? she called. She was trying to approach the temple yet it seemed to slip away from her, into the silver mists.

I am your sister Jola. I am the goddess Diba. You must find the strength to come to me and to be one with me, Fachalana. Then none may stand against thee.

I will try. She was nearing the doors now but a towering shadow, blacker than any night she had known, lay between her and the temple.

She could not pass it. Her father was too powerful.

I would not harm you, my child.

I know, Father. But she feared him, none the less, as she fell into the embrace of his mind.

Fachalana felt his astonishment as he read her secrets. And his emotions provided a door for her and she was able to follow them into Radal's own mind and read there.

You know my secrets now, Father, but I know yours.

Perhaps it was fair trade, for Fachalana now knew that Lord Radal would never again be able to do what he had done to her. She knew how to block his way.

With a word, she did, awakening in the little house in Ros-town.

~ ~ ~

"There is a body of men across the river," observed Habidros.

Sorsen turned his back to the dawn and peered into the distance. "Indeed there is. I can not make them out well from here." The son of Orgelo pulled a long metal cylinder from a leather tube that hung from his saddle. Sir Habidros had wondered about that odd holster.

"Perhaps my sighting tube will help." Sorsen put one end to his eye. "Ah, the colors are those of Count Mussago. The sun is catching them now."

The Cuddonian recognized the device, a simple tube with a black interior that helped the eye make out objects at a distance. He had seen them attached to rifles back in the Siphic states.

"I have heard," said Sir Sorsen, slipping the tube back into its scabbard, "that the Coradeans are now placing a glass lens at either end of these instruments and greatly increasing their efficacy."

"It is a large party, sir," said Habidros, more interested in matters at hand than what was being invented across the sea. "Larger than ours, I think."

"If they are Mussago's rabble, it hardly matters," replied Sorsen. "But that is not to dismiss them. It is odd that the count would send out so large a troop."

"The ferry is on our side, Sir Sorsen. Shall we go over and ask them their purpose?"

The leader of their company thought only a moment before making a decision. "You go, Sir Habidros, and take a couple men at arms with you. I shall remain here with our company." He slapped his comrade on the back. "I trust you to deal wisely. " Sorsen knew his second in command was more skillful in such things than he.

Four oarsmen steered the modest barge into the broad stream The

73

current was somewhat sluggish at this time of year and they crossed without great effort. An hour later, the ferry made a return to the east side of the Weldar.

His two men stepped from the vessel but Habidros was not with them, a leathery stranger having accompanied them in his stead. One of the soldiers handed Sorsen a note.

Sir, it read, *we agreed to an exchange to show our mutual good will and faith. I will remain here and Count Mussago's son will ride with you.* Sorsen looked up. Yes, he did remember the man from one official visit or another. He read on. *Officially, the younger Mussago is on a state visit, accompanied by men of his household. However, many of those across the river are soldiers of Sharsh. I know their commander.*

We have agreed to progress in parallel to Ros-town, each on our side of the river, where one can keep the other in view. I did warn them that there might be a chance that you would need to turn aside and pursue bandits at some point. If so, Mussago is to wave the banner he carries.

Again he looked at his guest. A long cloth of white was wound over one shoulder and tied at his waist. "Very well, Sir Mussago," said Sorsen. "You might as well have the horse of Captain Habidros."

"Master Mussago," replied the nobleman. Mussago had a low opinion of knighthood and of honors in general.

~ ~ ~

"Benawis is a traitor! He serves my father." These were Fachalana's first words on awakening from her trance. It was morning, though it seemed to her that she had only been gone a few minutes.

"I will tend to him," growled Guesare.

"Now," said the noblewoman, "before he receives warning. Father can speak to him from a distance."

"He is a wizard? We must deal with him."

Jobareth was already scribbling a note. "Take this," he said, "it will explain your mission to the guards and Lord Doufan." Guesare gave it a cursory look and stuffed it into his belt pouch.

"I shall come with you," said Ansa. "Fachalana will be well taken care of."

Within two minutes they had armed and outfitted themselves and were out the door. Their horses were at the nearby livery stable — the pair should soon be riding for the embassy.

Ansa silently said a prayer to the Great Sky as she hurried away. She could not remember the last time she had prayed, and certainly not to the primal deity of her people. It was not a prayer for her friend; it was a prayer for vengeance.

"Jobo," whispered Fachalana. He came close and knelt by her. "I could not hide my secrets from my father. He wrested the knowledge of Ros's paternity from me."

"It does not matter, Lana. How could he use it?"

"I do not know. But I fear he will find a way."

13

Modareth and the Princess Carrana would attend the theater tomorrow night. It was at Carrana's insistence that they were going; the prince had no great interest in the stage and would have preferred that both stayed safely home.

So would Pol. He might no longer be Prince Modareth's constant companion but his protection was still his concern. Now, he stood in the shadows across the street from the theater. It was still early in the day and there was little traffic in this district of the city.

He was watching three men. Two seemed stagehands; they had slipped out of a side door minutes earlier to meet with the third, a fellow in a long gray tunic. That tunic aroused Pol's suspicions. He remembered the description of a suspicious man in Dor who had so dressed.

Not that this trio were not suspicious enough on their own. Why would they meet out here in the street? If their business were legitimate, they would have gone inside.

That was a little thing, true, but enough for Pol. He decided to follow the man after he left the pair at the theater. It was easy to remain unseen, even though the young knight had no training in spy-craft — the fellow seemed quite oblivious to his surroundings.

In a shabbier neighborhood, the man entered one of a row of houses and did not reappear, although his shadow waited nearly an hour. He must have rooms there, surmised Pol.

Pol had met men here in Celatas, ruthless men who served the king's interests and would gladly pay his suspect a visit. He would go see one of them today.

And tomorrow, he would be sure to keep an eye out for those other two at the theater.

~ ~ ~

Benawis knew that Radal cared not for him and that his usefulness to his master was at an end. Yet he had warned him. Come to me if you can, he had said.

Perhaps if he could make his way to the sorcerer lord he might serve still in some way. What else was there for him? His career in Sharsh's diplomatic corps was gone. Sharsh itself was gone; he could not go home.

Benawis believed in his own abilities. There was nothing he could not accomplish in this world of hapless fools, who existed only so he might use them. Wherever he might escape to, he would make a success of it. Maybe he would just turn his back on Radal and this whole situation and head down to Morparas. It was said to be a good place for a man such as himself.

He gathered together a few belongings and threw them into a bag. Before anyone here was aware of his betrayals he would slip out of the embassy and disappear.

There was a bustle below. Had the news reached here already? The secretary hurried down the back stairs and through a door into the stables.

A guard blocked his way. "We've orders to stop you, sir."

Benawis, without a moment's pause, slipped his dagger between the man's ribs. Good fortune — a horse, already saddled, stood ready to ride. A slender boy loitered near it, one of the stable-hands, no doubt.

He brandished his bloody blade. "Out of my way, boy, or you'll get the same!" Benawis turned to mount Guesare's horse, first tossing his bag across its back.

Wound about her waist, beneath her belt, Ansa carried a bow string. Any Ani bowman would have an extra ready at hand in this manner. Yet any would also know that it had a second purpose. With an economy born of practice, she slipped the string from its hiding place and around the man's neck.

A few moments later, Guesare and a pair of guardsmen burst through the door. He looked at the man on the floor, his wide dead eyes staring into the void, and then at Ansa.

"Did you not think my brother would train me in such things?" asked she.

~ ~ ~

"There is little pleasure in my life these days, Donni."

Donzalo said nothing. He knew how things were but he knew not how to comfort Lomela.

The princess attempted to lighten their conversation. "Ros is getting larger every day. He reminds me of someone."

"Best not say that around Bolos, my lady."

She nodded soberly. "He is jealous of you anyway."

"There is little I can do about that, Lomela. We are each who we are." He gave her a smile. "I can think of reasons I might be jealous of my brother."

"There is nothing there to be jealous of these days. I fear Bolos has grown to distrust me as he does everyone else. He is becoming a stranger to me.

"I feel all alone these days. I pray that you will not leave me, Donzalo. I pray to all my gods and even to yours."

He took her in his arms. He had loved her once, with all the fervor of a first love, but knew he did no longer. But Donzalo cared greatly still for the Lady Lomela.

"I may have no choice but to leave, my princess. But know that I will always return."

~ ~ ~

The head of King Lareth's secret police in Celatas was a small, rotund man named Gos. Whether he had a title to go with his name, none of his subordinates knew. It was a secret police, after all.

He stood before both the royal princes now. "Sir Pol was correct about the man," said he. "Most definitely a sorcerer and there were papers that clearly incriminated him." He shook his head. "A bit of an amateur, I must say."

"Is he Partanacan?" asked Gawis.

"No, my lord, he is a man of Sharsh. Recently recruited, most likely, for his, um, skills."

That sounded logical to Modareth. "You said there were accomplices?"

"Yes, sir. We have questioned him quite thoroughly and he gave up names. We will be watching for the two assassins at the theater. Perhaps, my lord," he hesitated slightly, then continued, "you should not attend."

"My wife would be terribly disappointed. But perhaps so." A question then occurred to the prince. "But how will you catch them if there is no one there for them to assassinate? Or attempt to assassinate, I should say!"

"Sir Pol has some thoughts on that, my lord," responded the little spy-master with a sly smile.

~ ~ ~

What could he do with his new knowledge? wondered Radal. That Donzalo was the father of Lomela's child was momentous, indeed, but would be near impossible to prove. It could most certainly provide the wedge he desired to drive between the brothers.

But there were ways to suggest it to Bolos. He could send dreams, after a fashion, to the man, images that would enter his sleep and haunt his days. Not if he were drunk, though; then his mind would not be receptive.

So the whole premise on which he and Lareth had originally plotted against Donzalo's life had been wrong. That had been the secret Fachalana had told the king.

Lord Radal briefly thought of his spy Benawis. Had the man escaped? He had little talent and was probably of no more use as a tool, but Radal had learned not to throw tools away.

He would prefer he not be questioned, as well.

Fachalana. He would never again be able to reach her as he had. The sorcerer marveled at his daughter's strength, her ability to read him as he had read her, when their minds had occupied the same space.

He hoped that what she had read of her father's soul would not be too much for her to bear. It was nearly too much for him. Too often, now, he saw doors open to him that he had hoped to keep closed. Too often, they beckoned him into ways from which he knew he could never return.

The Fay had not been able to aid Fachalana, but there had been some other, hadn't there? He had sensed it only but knew it had almost provided her with a refuge where he could not follow. And that other had seemed, in some way, familiar to him.

It was time to call all his men to him here at this tower. It was time to go destroy not only Donzalo but the man's world and those he loved.

14

The ride north was uneventful. Blen found his Cuddonian guest an entertaining companion on their journey; Sorsen did not have the same experience with the silent Mussago. Both troops, in time, found themselves on the outskirts of Rostown, those of Count Mussago and Sharsh on the west, the company from County Arvaram on the east. These latter stopped just below the mouth of the Abam to make their camp. To reach Ros-town itself, they would need go upstream a short distance to where a narrow bridge carried the Great Road across this lesser stream. Heavier traffic went further up yet to a place it might be forded.

"Make camp here," Sir Blen told his contingent, halting by an open field just south of the town. "I shall go across and see what the intentions of Sorsen and Mussago might be."

He, Habidros, and two men at arms — he felt it diplomatic to choose one each from his own troops and those of Mussago — took the ferry across the Weldar.

Mussago and Sorsen awaited them on the shore, having left the Arvaram men encamped.

"The first thing," said Sir Sorsen, once the group had repaired to a nearby tavern, "is to go pay a visit to the count. He surely did not expect our troops to arrive without notice. We have sent a man ahead to announce both myself and Master Mussago. Then," he said, "we must have a council about all of this."

"I'd best not accompany you to Borrago's, I mean Bolos's, keep," stated Blen. "He knows me as part of the Sharshite embassy, not a soldier in your father's service, Master Mussago." He gave a little bow to the man who gravely returned it.

"I am not sure how Count Bolos feels about me," said Habidros.

"Nor am I," said Sir Blen. "You might better return to your own camp." Sorsen nodded his agreement. "I shall ride with you a way, however, gentlemen. I should report to the ambassador before I take further action."

THE HAND OF THE SORCERER

~ ~ ~

"I do not understand why these companies of men have suddenly appeared." Bolos ceased pacing and sank heavily into a chair. "Mussago and Sorsen, arriving separately but coming here together, both expressing vague concerns about rumors they have heard."

"Perhaps the rumors they have heard were about each other," suggested Lady Lomela.

"Indeed, my lady! I think they trust each other not at all." He turned toward his brother, standing on the other side of the room and seeming to idly look out the window. "You were recently at Orgelo's, Donzalo. Did you hear aught there?"

"Nothing much at Orgelo's. But Count Mussago seemed to have some concerns." He did not feel inclined to mention the presence of Sir Blen and Sharshite troops there.

"The two are rivals," observed Sir Corgos. "If one took action, the other was bound to do the same."

Bolos nodded. "Let us hope the process does not continue with every count in Lama."

All four thought on that for a little while.

Then Bolos again spoke. "I hear too of strange incidents at the Sharshite embassy. One of their diplomats murdered and a guardsman sorely wounded!

"On top of that, Sir Blen seems to have returned and is friendly with Sorsen and Mussago."

Sir Corgos replied, "The ambassador claims that the slain man was a spy and assassin and that he wounded the guard. I have learned from some of the staff there that he was the secretary to the legate. I have also heard that he was most expertly garroted by someone."

"That is the Anian way," observed Donzalo. Both he and Lomela thought of their friend Ansa. Could one of her countrymen be here? Neither knew that the woman herself had returned.

"I would doubt that there are any Anians in the embassy," said Corgos, "but none of the servants seem to know just who did it."

"I am certain Lord Doufan knows," Lomela said. "And I am just as certain he will never tell you."

~ ~ ~

Pol of Arolin could scarce keep from laughing. He stood in the shadowed rear of the royal box, while two of Gos's men, in the guises of Prince Modareth and his wife Carrana, sat watching the play.

To his eyes, they looked ridiculous. For those in the darkened theater, the deception probably worked well enough.

Although his attention was directed elsewhere, he could not help occasionally hearing bits of dialog from the stage. I could write better than that, he thought.

There was a signal from the other side of the hall, a man draping a red cloak over the front of his box. Something was happening. His two companions had seen it as well and put their hands to the hilts of their daggers. They would use them only if absolutely necessary and attempt to keep up this charade. Those in the theater might never even realize anything had happened.

Pol stepped deeper into shadow. The assassins would know there was a guard in the box but there was no reason to make him easy to see. Slowly, stealthily, the door was opened and a pair, dressed as ordinary stagehands and brandishing short swords, entered. The knight hoped that Gos's minions were close behind these two — Pol had no desire to engage in a sword fight this evening.

He stepped boldly out before them, sword in hand, hoping to create a moment of confusion as their attention went from their intended victims to him. Their sword points wavered. It was time enough for several burly policemen to enter and lay hands on the pair and drag them away with minimum fuss.

Then Sir Pol took a chair and tried to enjoy the remainder of the play. However, he found far too many things to criticize.

~ ~ ~

"I still feel weak," complained Fachalana.

"A weak Fachalana is still stronger than most women," replied her friend Ansa. "Give it a day and you'll be out challenging men to duels."

"I hope so. I know my body will grow stronger. But there was so much darkness in his mind, Ansa. I do not know if I can contain it all."

The Anian did not know how to answer that. And found she did not need to for Jobareth Nafal and the minstrel Guesare came into the room.

"How is our Lady Fachalana?" asked the diplomat.

"She feels weak," responded Ansa, giving him a look that clearly said to ask no more.

Jobareth accordingly broached another subject. "I think it is time that Sir Jan and his esquire disappeared. Lord Doufan would like me to invite the Ladies Fachalana and Maresta to come and stay with us for a while."

"Won't it seem as though we suddenly appeared in County Rosam without crossing its borders?" asked Ansa.

"We can claim you were with Sir Blen's company. In the confusion of bringing some three-score men across the border, might not a pair of demure ladies have been overlooked?"

"It's plausible enough," agreed Guesare. "Blen will go along with it?"

"He suggested it once Lord Doufan told him of the ladies' presence here." Nafal gave the women a look that seemed filled with questions. "Sir Blen seems quite concerned about our ladies."

"We spent much time together," murmured Fachalana.

The butler entered with a tray and a pitcher of wine. "Thank you," said Jobareth. "Just leave it."

"A good man," commented Guesare and then suggested a quite different destination for the pair. "My ladies, why not accompany me to Sir Paren's? It would be a better place to rest and you would be far from the eyes of Bolos and his spies.

Ansa nodded. "In time, maybe. Are you leaving soon?"

"Sir Paren hasn't named a day but I think he will not wait much longer. He would like to be home for Autumn Feast."

"I think we should accept Lord Doufan's gracious invitation," said Lady Fachalana. "If we wish to go further in time, it is a good starting point." She sat up on the couch and continued, "And I would very much like to visit Lomela. It's time she knew we were here!"

~ ~ ~

There had been a camp here, a large one, and for quite some time. They had gone no more than a day or two ago.

A filthy bunch, too. There was no military discipline among them, thought Perdos. These were brigands. They might be the men who had followed Sojel.

Gone where? East, he could see. There was no point in following their trail; he was not concerned with them right now, though he would gladly see every man of them swinging from a gallows.

And down the road a good distance, another camp, a new one. He had seen them arrive and recognized the colors and insignia of Count Orgelo. He also recognized the tall Cuddonian who had ridden in soon after, another of Guesare's brothers.

As to the minstrel's whereabouts, he was uncertain. He had heard that he was being seen around town, plying his trade. Perdos was unwelcome in Ros-town or he might have simply found the man and challenged him. But if the town guards laid hands on him, he might never find another chance.

It was much too far to see the Rosam keep from here. He had spent some good times there, he and his brother. Perdos felt a momentary nostalgia.

Maybe Bolos would lift the ban on him, let him return from exile. His former employer had always treated him well.

Ah, but that was a time that would not return. Perdos had other dreams now and they did not include serving in a nobleman's guard. And first, he must settle matters with Guesare.

15

"My father told me to leave things to your discretion, Blen. But if you take an action that I feel we can not support, I will withdraw my men and my authority."

He's probably been working on that speech, thought Habidros. But it is a quite sensible statement to make.

"Certainly, Master Mussago. If I need to take drastic actions, I shall do so in the name of King Lareth, not your father."

That seemed to satisfy the man, who added no more to their debate.

Habidros himself had no voice at all in this council, other than to make suggestions. It was up to Blen and Sorsen to come to decisions here.

"We should remain in our current locations," Sorsen felt. "At another time, I might have encamped my men outside the walls of Keep Rosam but I fear that would make Bolos nervous."

"That it might," said Sir Blen. "So each of us would be separated from Ros-town by water. Although," he added, "you can cross yours more quickly."

"Then come over and join us," Habidros suggested.

Sorsen nodded approval. "It would reassure the count that we are not about to start a war in his front yard.

"And, after all, we are here for the same reason. We are concerned about what is going on here and the plans of certain — traitors." Sorsen had been fully filled in on the part of Lord Radal in the situation. This did not mean that he suddenly trusted Sharsh.

"Very well," agreed Blen. "I shall send our men over a few at a time." He gave a quick glance at Mussago. The man seemed to have no objections.

"By the way, Sir Sorsen, did you ever catch up to any of those outlaws?"

"We did not, Sir Blen. There are rumors that they have ridden east toward the Cuddon."

"Sir Paren should know if they are passing near his keep," said Habidros. "He may want to return with his company."

"I shall tell him when I visit the count tomorrow," Sorsen promised. "But he has a good master of arms up there to take care of things in his absence."

~ ~ ~

His men were on the march. They should reach him here on the edge of the Cuddon in a day or two.

Radal was weary. His struggle with his daughter had taken much from him but he had not rested. There was too much else to be dealt with, both in this world and others.

And magic always took its toll.

The sorcerer had been sending dreams to Count Bolos. These dreams were not fully formed but, rather, suggestions. The count's own mind would provide the details. He could not make Bolos believe things he did not already suspect, somewhere deep in his soul. Radal would feed those suspicions and fears, make them grow strong, make them a fever that consumed the man.

He had what he had read in Fachalana's mind to thank for the directions he turned those dreams.

By the time he moved westward with his followers, Count Bolos might be ready to welcome him as a friend — the only friend left in a world that had betrayed him.

~ ~ ~

He had found Lomela weeping. He did not know why she wept; there were too many possibilities these days. Donzalo simply took her into his arms and asked no questions.

So they were when his brother entered the room.

Bolos was quite obviously drunk. "Slut of Sharsh!" he snarled. "First going behind my back with your dandy Nafal and now my own brother."

The princess was taken aback. There was enough truth in what he had said to stun her into a momentary silence.

"There is nothing between the lady and myself," said Donzalo. "I only comforted her as a friend."

"Do not trust her, Donni," was the count's slurred response. He looked at his brother. "Why should I even trust you?"

"Bolos!" Lomela stepped forward and took her husband's arm. In his anger he shook her off and the Lady Lomela fell to the floor. He stared for a moment as Donzalo stooped to assist her in rising.

"Leave my wife alone. Leave her where she belongs." He slapped his brother fully across the face and turned with outstretched hand, as if he would do the same to his wife.

A massive fist met with Bolos's jaw.

"I am sorry, my brother," Donzalo said, helping Bolos to his feet.

Sir Corgos burst into the room, followed by a pair of guardsmen. An attendant had run to him as soon as it had seemed there might be trouble. He looked from the solicitous Donzalo to the count, rubbing his jaw.

"Place my brother under arrest," ordered Count Bolos.

"Arrest, my lord?" The master of arms was astounded.

"Yes, yes." Bolos seemed suddenly unsure of himself. "Confine him to his quarters. I'll think on how to deal with this later." He stared at his wife for a moment, without expression, and then stumbled from the room.

The young knight silently accompanied the older one down to his own rooms.

"I will not lock you in, Donzalo, but there will be guards outside your door. Do not try to get by them," warned Corgos.

"Certainly, Sir Corgos. You have my promise."

"And that is good enough for me, Sir Donzalo."

The young man sat a while in his room, pondering.

Why should he wait here? At best, his brother would banish him so he might as well do that himself. Everyone might be better off that way. Donzalo went to the hidden panel in his quarters.

I'd best make sure this is well concealed, he told himself, and dragged a chest close to the wall before entering. Then he pulled it against the wall from within the passage and slid the panel closed. Down to the cave in the cliffs he went, and out into the night.

In the darkness, he groped his way along the ledge, clinging to the cliff wall. Thank Kamat it is not raining, he said to himself.

His pathway widened and Donzalo saw trees ahead, scrubby pines rooted into a rubble of rock and sparse soil. On their far side, a gentler slope allowed him to descend — still with care — to the base of the cliffs.

He stood on the more level ground and looked up at the way he had come, the sheer black face of the cliffs more a shadow than a tangible object. Could he ever return as he had promised Lomela?

There was a man near him. He could barely make out his form by the light of the stars. Donzalo drew his sword — he had kept one in his chamber and had made sure to strap it on before leaving. "Who is there?" he asked.

"A good evening to you, Sir Donzalo," said Oder.

OF DREAMS: THE TENTH TALE

1

"Gone? How could this be?"

Sir Corgos shook his head. "I know not, my lord. The guard was outside his door and saw naught."

"They must have been bribed. You will question them and find who is behind this." Count Bolos glared at his master of arms, his frustration obvious.

Corgos did not believe his men had been corrupted. Not that they couldn't be but it would mean that someone in the keep had turned not only Donzalo's guards but also the soldiers at the gates into traitors in a matter of hours. That seemed unlikely, to say the least.

But he could find no other explanation.

Not one soul had seen Donzalo since the master of arms himself had closed his door on him. Questioning would do little good now; men must be sent out into town and countryside to search. He would dispatch a messenger to the captain of the garrison down in Ros-town to be on the lookout.

The count had his own personal network of spies, too. Sir Corgos knew this. Donzalo would have done well to travel quickly and far. Best the boy leave all this behind and find peace somewhere.

It would all settle down soon, anyway. Count Bolos had greater concerns than the whereabouts of his younger brother. Even if that younger brother did fell him with a blow to the jaw.

He probably didn't even hit him that hard, thought Corgos. If Donzalo had put his full force into his punch, Bolos might never have gotten up.

But when all this had blown over, one question would remain: how did the boy get out of his guarded quarters?

~ ~ ~

Sir Jan and his attendant Saj had gone across the river. Lady Fachalana and her companion Maresta had returned in the company of Sir Blen.

As they rode up to the embassy, Blen was intrigued to hear their tale of the successes of the young soldier he had left in his stead, back in Dor. "Sir Pol, it is? I knew the boy had potential but did not expect him to rise so quickly."

"Pol has been a most fortunate lad," opined Fachalana.

"It was not just luck that brought Pol here to his posting in Lama. I picked the men that came with us and he had already proven himself bright and dependable.

"And I chose to send him with Jobareth to Mountain Keep when he asked for a good man as an attendant. Though it seems to me," he mused, "that Pol seemed eager to volunteer for that duty."

"He saw an opportunity for advancement," said Ansa. "Nothing complicated there."

"Or maybe he was just sick of guard duty in Ros-town," Blen replied. "Either way, he was out to change his fortunes."

"I don't like this horse," complained Fachalana, "nor this saddle." Her knightly steed had remained behind at Mussago's camp and she was riding sidesaddle for the first time in weeks.

"I'll see about getting your own horse over to you in a while. To come riding back on Sir Jan's mount would have been suspicious."

"But I fear you must continue to ride sidesaddle," said Ansa. "It is expected of you."

Ansa boldly straddled her horse, as no one had any expectations at all about her.

"I hope to ride no mount for some time," sighed Fachalana, "other than a feather bed."

~ ~ ~

King Lareth held two letters, dated a few days apart. Both were from Lord Doufan and both concerned the Lady Fachalana.

He had been amused by the first, telling how the ladies had arrived incognito in County Rosam. Lareth tried to picture them accoutered as fighting men and found it not that difficult. He knew Fachalana well.

The second had been alarming. So the lady had inherited her father's abilities? This helped explain a number of small things about which he had wondered. It also told him that Lord Radal was still actively seeking to take the life of Donzalo Rosam.

Would it matter if he did? Yes, Donzalo was the father of Lomela's child, the child prophesied to rule in Lama, but it would not do for that paternity to be discovered. Kings must sometimes be cynical, he told himself.

But most of all, kings must not act rashly. He would let things play out as they would in Lama and take action only if necessary.

~ ~ ~

Bolos knew he had acted badly. The count truly wished that Donzalo had not fled, however he had accomplished it. They would have smoothed all this over when they had both cooled down in the morning.

He liked to think that he would have dealt leniently with his brother and sent him packing off to Uncle Paren's with orders to stay away a good long while.

The count rubbed at his sore jaw. Yes, he would sign an official order to just that effect. If Donzalo wished to return, then, he would need fear nothing. But one way or another, he did not want his brother here in the keep again.

He had been wrong to doubt his wife, hadn't he? Yet in his dreams, he saw her in Donzalo's arms, and their embrace was not innocent.

They were dreams. They meant nothing. He must apologize to Lomela. He had never laid hands on her so before. It was the wine that did it.

Bolos vowed to take never another drink while he lived and he did not. But he still had disturbing dreams.

93

~ ~ ~

"We of the Ani — those of us who are spies — know of that passage below Keep Rosam. We built it, after all."

"So I had assumed," said Donzalo, "I and Sir Copago."

"He showed it to you?"

The young Laman nodded. "And he had learned of it from our father. Who told him, I've no idea."

"Your grandfather, Count Ros. He learned of the way through bribery and used it to capture the keep. How did you think he came into possession of so formidable a fortress?" The Anian spy's tone was only very slightly sarcastic.

Donzalo ignored that. It was to be expected that the Ani would still find their expulsion from Lama a bit of a sore spot. "Then he gained a keep in much the same way his father lost Mountain Keep to King Greneth — treachery." He poked at the campfire for a few seconds. "That is one of those two-edged swords that appear in so many proverbs, isn't it?"

"I suppose it is, my friend," replied Oder, "or something similar. Have you any thoughts as to where you might go?" They sat now looking out over a valley of small farms, well to the northeast of Castle Rosam. Donzalo wasn't sure whether this area was part of his uncle's jurisdiction.

Donzalo shrugged. "My friend Daboreth would welcome me. Probably Orgelo would, too, but I am not sure I would want to be in his hands."

"Nor would I," agreed Oder, with a smile.

"I could head for yon hills." Donzalo nodded toward the east. "And return to the Cuddon. I suppose I could even go to Sharsh now that King Lareth no longer wants my blood."

"Ah, but for what purpose?"

"None, I suppose. I don't know that I have any purpose now."

"You have friends for whom you care. That, I think, should be your purpose." Oder, who had been staring into the fire, lifted his eyes. "Did you know that my sister was in County Rosam?"

94

"Ansa? Is she there at your bidding?"

"No. She and Lady Fachalana can create enough plots of their own, these days."

2

"I may follow you in a short time, Sir Paren, I and the ladies."

"You are always welcome in my home, Guesare, as are the Lady Fachalana and her companion. I know not why they would want to visit our quiet manor."

"Fachalana needs quiet for a time. If we come, I shall give you the whole story as to why." The minstrel spoke on, lowering his voice. "I have heard news of Donzalo. He is safely with a friend of mine."

"Then tell that friend to send the boy to me. Bolos is willing to forget the entire business if Donzalo remains at my keep."

They rode slowly along, Sir Paren's men following. Guesare had felt it wise not to enter Keep Rosam and had joined the reeve's group as they began their journey home. "I would feel better if the women had an escort to my estate. Perhaps I should leave some men with you."

"You need all of them with you, sir. I have heard the reports of lawless men across the Abam." Guesare remained silent for a while, then said, "Donni is concerned about the Lady Lomela."

"I think Bolos frightened himself. Oh, I have seen him like this before, seen him mistreat and slap servants since he was a boy. It has always been the result of drunkenness.

"Bolos is not a violent man when sober and he is trying very hard to stay sober."

"Drink only brings out who we truly are," was Guesare's opinion. "Give my greetings to all at your keep." He turned and rode back toward Ros-town.

~ ~ ~

One would not be incorrect to say that Radal was pleased by the news from Castle Rosam. It is possible that he even smiled. Donzalo was out in the open again and more vulnerable. The phantasms he had sent to haunt Bolos's sleep had proven effective.

He would continue to trouble the man's dreams, but it was now time for more than that — time to leave the Cuddon, to move his force closer to the keep and prepare to act directly. They would ride on the morrow.

As others, he was puzzled by Donzalo's escape. He knew it could not be magic, as gossip around Ros-town had it. Magic did not work that way. Were it so simple, Radal would not have needed to summon a dragon to carry him from Mountain Keep.

Yes, he had once sent the Hounds of Asak from one world to another to destroy young Donzalo but a part of them remained tethered to that other realm. They were never completely here, existing in two worlds at once. If the men of Castle Rosam should ever dig where they thought they had buried the beasts, they might be surprised to find no trace left.

The other news did not much move the sorcerer one way or another. Benawis had been killed trying to flee the embassy. Death was always a good way to tie up loose ends. The circumstances of that death did interest him. It suggested that there were unknown players in this game.

And he knew now that his daughter's friend Maresta — no, her name was Ansa — was an Anian spy. Radal had almost overlooked this bit of knowledge amid all the rest he had read in Fachalana's mind.

He should have paid more attention to that little girl.

~ ~ ~

"Bolos was actually quite happy to hear you were here. I believe he hopes it will cheer up his wife. He feels guilty enough that he would allow her pretty much anything at the moment.

"Moreover, it helped dispel any suspicions he had about my own arrival — I was simply escorting you from Sharsh and we rode here with Mussago's men for the protection they afforded."

"That does leave a few days unaccounted for," Ansa pointed out. "Where does he think we were between your arrival and ours?"

"Tired and resting in Mussago's tents," replied Blen. "It's believable enough."

"And now tired and resting in the embassy of Sharsh," said Lady Fachalana. "Bolos will think us extraordinarily exhausted." Fachalana was propped up on many pillows in her bed; Ansa sat at the foot of it while Blen occupied a chair nearby.

"Are you, my lady?" asked the knight. "Jobareth suggested that you had undergone some great trial."

"I'm not even sure how much you know, anymore, Sir Blen, we have kept so many secrets from so many people. You learned that we came to County Rosam in disguise, no?" She furrowed her brow momentarily. "Well, of course you did."

"Yes. Nafal filled me in on all that I had not learned already from the ambassador."

Fachalana turned her eyes toward her traveling companion. "Your secrets are yours to keep or to tell, Maresta."

"If you are going to tell all, then so shall I," decided the Anian. Fachalana nodded her assent to that.

"Sir Blen, most of our friends here already are aware of this, including Jobareth Nafal — my true name is Ansa and I am Ani. I am a spy. I am also the Lady Fachalana's loyal friend."

Blen raised his eyebrows. "I should be more surprised, I am sure." He turned to the viscountess. "Can you top that?"

"I am a sorceress," replied Fachalana. "Will that do?"

"I believe so, my lady." He looked at her long and thoughtfully. "I have seen what the practice of magic can do to your father. Is that what wearies you now?"

"In a way. I don't think I'm up to telling the story, Ansa. Why don't you?"

So Ansa did, recounting their entire tale from the time Blen had left them in Dor. Before she was half-done, the weary Fachalana had fallen asleep.

"It was not only the struggle with her father that so weakened her," Ansa finished, "but dealing with all his dark memories that are now within her. She finds herself drifting and dreaming, Blen, and I fear Fachalana may lose herself."

"And we would lose Fachalana," whispered Blen. "That can not happen."

"No. But what are we to do? What are we to do?"

~ ~ ~

"If you persist in saving my life, my father will have to award you some sort of title."

"Knighthood is sufficient, my lord," said Sir Pol. "I think having a title might be quite wearisome."

"It is," agreed Prince Modareth. "I would as soon be a lecturer at the university." This office of his might make one think him just such, thought Pol, with its untidy stacks of books and manuscripts.

"And I, sir, have given thought to turning my hand to the writing of a play."

"Our friend Gos would rather see you enter his service."

"Our Pol a policeman? Surely not," objected Princess Carrana.

"More a spy, my lady," said Pol. "I do think I could readily combine the two."

"You could," agreed Modareth, "But if you are to be a spy, I would prefer you were mine." He rushed on, as he tended to do when he felt awkward about something. "I need men I can trust around me. This is one thing the last year has taught me."

Carrana smiled. She thought she had taught her husband a few things since their marriage.

An idea came to her. "Couldn't we order Lady Fachalana's theater reopened in her absence? Pol might run it for her until she returns."

"Hmm, I think Father would not object. He did order Lord Radal's villa sealed but this isn't the same."

Pol laughed. "I know nothing of operating a theater, my lord." Then, on giving it a moment's thought, he added, "I must admit, though, it would provide an excellent base of operations."

"It's better than letting it sit empty," decided the prince. "We can always hire someone to actually manage the theater, as Maresta did for Fachalana."

"Very well, my lord and lady, I am willing to try it. But you must come to my opening!"

"We would not miss it," promised Princess Carrana.

~ ~ ~

"We are not far now from where we first met," said Oder. As they had climbed into the the Cuddon, the forests had thinned and now the hills about them were, for the most part, barren of trees. They were still green at this time of year, and many flowers yet bloomed, golds and yellows spreading across the upland meadows.

"The weather is certainly better."

"I do not intend to linger sufficiently long in the Cuddon to see it change," replied the Anian. "I need only visit one of our houses here, to send messages and see if any await me."

"The business of spies," said Donzalo.

"Indeed. We spend more time sending letters back and forth than aught else." Oder smiled and spoke on. "I could have taken you and Guesare there that night, rather than camping in the cold and snow. But I would not have trusted you with its location, then."

"The Cuddonians do not mind your presence here?"

"Remember that the area still has allegiance to our empire. It is old, the agreement between the nobles of the Cuddon and we Ani — they give lip-service to the emperor as their overlord and we leave them alone, mostly, and promise to keep Lama from pressing upon their borders."

Donzalo knew of that agreement. It had saved the Anians from spending resources on a costly invasion of these hills while they had swept west into Lama, Sharsh, and even Lorj. Since, the Cuddon had served as a useful buffer between them and Lama.

"We may rest there a short while," continued Oder. "Then I think it best to travel back toward your own home. Perhaps your uncle's keep should be our destination."

What might await him there? wondered Donzalo. Would he be welcome? He had half a mind to turn north to Drolwym rather than follow this spy with his own secret agenda.

But Oder was right. His friends were what gave purpose to his life now. If he had any destiny at all, it would be found there.

3

Dovolo rode beside his master. He had never before had occasion to interact personally with Lord Radal and did so with some trepidation. Yet the sorcerer seemed affable enough and willing to converse.

Radal, having closed himself in his tower for quite some time with none to speak to but a few most ignorant ruffians, was pleased to have a more intelligent companion at his side. He commented to him now and again on things they passed along the road.

The sergeant, emboldened, posed a question to Lord Radal. "Sir, is it true you rode here upon a dragon?"

"I did."

"Did it breathe fire, my lord?"

Radal was amused enough for a small smile, the first in many weary days. "A common misconception. The fire, in fact, comes from the other end of the beast."

"They — *fart* fire?" The man was incredulous.

"In a manner of speaking. It is not truly fire but a corrosive liquid, such as a skunk projects. Indeed, most knowledgeable natural philosophers believe the dragon to be a member of the weasel tribe."

Dovolo had come of a good family, though his own estate had greatly fallen, and had a bit of schooling. He did not find this idea unbelievable.

But, never having seen a dragon — even one of the small ones — he was not inclined to accept it unquestioningly either. Not that it mattered right now.

They would cross the Abam soon. That would be when they were most vulnerable, most likely to be spied. Then on to the camp Sojel had established deep in the forest the year before, somewhat to the north and west of Sir Paren's keep.

Dovolo had not been there at the ill-fated attempt to take that small fortress, not having yet joined this troop, but had heard of it from those who were. Did Lord Radal now have some idea of taking Keep Rosam? They would be within a hard two days ride of it.

Well, he had his long sword slung over his back and would use it when the order came. No sense in worrying about things until then.

He took a sidelong look at the man beside him. Dressed, as ever, in black, the sorcerer was impossibly lean, almost skeletal, and had allowed his beard to grow since leaving Mountain Keep, starkly white against his dark, hollowed face. To the eyes of Dovolo, Lord Radal did not seem a well man.

Radal grew silent. This undertaking would soon end, one way or another. If he survived it, he knew he would not live long after. He was too spent, too dependent on the elixirs he brewed to keep himself going.

When all was done, Lareth might see that he still served his interests. Theirs had always been a single destiny, a fierce loyalty of one to the other. He had not forgotten that and neither, he was sure, had the king.

Before that, though, came his vengeance and the assurance of Fachalana's future. Nothing else truly mattered.

~ ~ ~

Ansa had come to County Rosam just after the Autumn Festival the previous year. She was not certain how it was celebrated here.

"This festival is, before all else," Jobareth Nafal told her, "a religious occasion. For Kamatians, who see the sun as a powerful symbol of their god, all the equinoxes and solstices are such.

"But it is also a celebration of the first fruits of the harvest. There will be a certain amount of dancing and drinking of cider."

"I hope we can get Lomela to dance," said Lady Fachalana.

"And you as well, Lana," Jobareth replied. "You seem much stronger."

"All I needed was a little rest." Fachalana did not mention that she now possessed the knowledge of certain drugs that her father had used. She had taken only a small dose; surely there had been no harm in that.

"I think it is time that Lomela knows about me. It seems everyone else in the world does!"

"Of our circle, only she and Donzalo are still in the dark. And who knows when we will see him again?" asked the diplomat.

103

"Guesare can send messages to him," said Ansa in a rather small voice. "He is with my brother." This was the first the others had heard of this.

"But," she continued, "I am fairly certain he already has some sense of your powers."

Yes, thought Fachalana, we saw each other in dream, on the silver plain. She could not seem to find that world again, though she had searched.

"Be that as it may," stated Nafal. "Count Bolos has made all of us welcome at the keep for this holiday. Yes, even me. Indeed, he asked me whether you might want to stay there for a time with his wife rather than live at the embassy."

"Why not?" said Fachalana. "I'll start packing."

~ ~ ~

Bolos had dreamed of the king. Lareth had stood over his body with bloody sword, while his daughter laughed in the arms of a face-less lover.

There was none to save him. He thought he saw familiar faces in the crowd that stood about, pointing and making jokes to one another. Orgelo? Copago? They might have been there.

A tall man, dark, no more than a shadow, whispered to him. *I can save you*, he said.

But Bolos was already dead, and soldiers looted and burned across his land.

He had dreamed too many such dreams lately. Doctor Heragos said they might be the result of his quitting of all drink, that the poisons were working their way out of him and the dreams might lessen in time. The count hoped so, fervently.

In his waking life, he could barely remember King Lareth. He had seen him only the once, when he had traveled to Mountain Keep to escort his bride home. Bolos could tell at the time that the man had a low opinion of him, that he felt his daughter was too good for him.

Maybe she was.

Not that it mattered now. They had done their duty, as should the children of power, and he had a healthy heir to show for it. Now he must try to preserve all that boy should someday inherit.

Bolos knew how fragile the balance was in Lama. It was not that long since his grandfather and the other counts had established it, having expelled the Ani. Who could expect it to last forever?

Who could expect it to last with enemies on all sides?

~ ~ ~

Jobareth decided to ask outright. "Did you have a secret way built in and out of the embassy?" The thought was on his mind since Donzalo's disappearance, which he felt certain had been through the passage he had seen.

Sir Blen chuckled. "Who whispered that rumor to you?"

"Donzalo, actually. Is there one or isn't there?"

"Yes and no, Legate. There is a passage of sorts but it is not at all secret. Follow."

He led Nafal to the hall outside the ambassador's rooms. "Do you know what lies directly beneath us?"

Jobareth thought a moment, laying out a floor plan in his mind. "The kitchens," he stated with some certainty.

"They are," agreed Blen. "After you had gone to fetch Lord Doufan here, I remembered the dumb waiters I had seen in Mountain Keep and had one added." He gestured toward a panel in the wall.

"I thought this was but a closet," Jobareth said. "Does it go up to the third floor?" Visions came to him of late meals being delivered to his room.

"It does. We were not keeping it secret. We have simply not used it yet.

"But there is a small secret about it ," he continued, opening the panel. "I decided that as long as it was here, there was no reason not to make it big enough for a man, if an emergency arose. See, there is a ladder, off there to the side." He pointed into the opening.

Jobareth inspected it, looking up and down the brick-walled shaft. "This could be handy. For both its purposes."

Blen shrugged. "The ambassador is not interested in using it. He prefers to go down to the kitchen to gossip with the cook when he wants a snack.

"Incidentally," he added, "it goes all the way to the roof. You may not have noticed that we have one chimney too many up there."

The legate made a mental note to look the next time he was outside. "I should speak to Lord Doufan. It might not be a bad idea for you to join me." He rapped at the ambassador's door, which was answered by his scribe. The man gave them a courteous nod of his head and ushered them in.

Doufan sat in a comfortable chair in a corner of his office, writing. "What can I do for you, gentlemen?" he asked, waving them toward nearby seats.

"My lord," began Jobareth, "the Lady Fachalana and Maresta are now settled in at Castle Rosam. I would expect them to stay for several days."

"Yes," said the ambassador. "And then what?"

"That is very much the question, sir. The ladies want to visit Sir Paren's keep in the company of Sir Guesare and I thought it might be wise were I to accompany them. If you can spare me, my lord."

"And if I permit them to go at all," responded Lord Doufan. "Sir Blen will have to ride away with those troops of his sooner or later. Would you leave me with neither of you here?"

"I think I can trust my second to lead our men back to Count Mussago's lands," said Blen. "Though, indeed, sooner or later I would have to go to them."

"Do you think Donzalo will show up at his uncle's?" asked Doufan.

"I think it is — possible," Jobareth said.

"I've not doubt the ladies think the same. I shall have to consider all this." He busied himself with the papers on his lapboard for a moment before speaking again to the two. "Are you attending the ball at the castle? I am quite looking forward to the evening."

"I am, of course, sir," replied Nafal. "And I shall be certain to drag Sir Blen along, no matter how much he may object!"

~ ~ ~

Perdos was, in a word, bored. It seemed that all he did was wait and, for the most part, wait alone.

He again considered riding boldly into Ros-town and standing outside the house where he knew Guesare was staying. Challenge him right there in the street and have done. But too much might go wrong and he would lose his chance forever.

Attempting to waylay him on the road would be just as risky, though he knew the minstrel sometimes rode alone up towards the castle. If it were further from town, maybe.

Perdos had ridden down to the soldiers' encampment south of the Abam one day. No one knew him there so he could gossip a while with those fellows, learn what was going on, enjoy some comradeship for an hour or two. Their number had swelled; apparently another group had joined them, one including a number of men from Sharsh.

They all seemed to get along together well enough and, like Perdos, were waiting. Their leaders seemed uncertain whether to stay or go.

"Sorsen is going to the ball up at the keep," one told him. "After that, maybe we'll ride home. We're going to have our own Autumn celebration here at the camp. Come on by and join us."

It was tempting, but Perdos knew he would be watching, not drinking, on the day of the equinox.

~ ~ ~

The line dividing life and death
is measured by a single breath.

THE HAND OF THE SORCERER

Exhale what is and all that might,
a wisp to fade into the night.

When next we breathe, what unknown air
fills souls now past all mortal care?

That dark divide breaks ev'ry bond;
breathe deeply ere you cross beyond.

"And that, gentlefolk, is the final soliloquy," announced Pol, lowering his manuscript. There was a moment of silence before Prince Modareth began applauding. His wife quickly joined in, followed by the others in attendance.

They don't understand it, thought Sir Pol. It was ridiculous to think he could write something.

"Will you open your season with this, Sir Pol?" asked the Baroness Ysena.

"No, my lady, I think something from repertory would be a better choice."

"But you must present it later in the season," said Modareth. "We need something new and fresh." The portly Princess Carrana, hanging on her husband's arm, nodded in agreement.

"I shall attempt it, sir." Perhaps they didn't hate the play after all. "It will need rewriting, I am sure, before it is presentable."

The opening should be within the month. Word had been given out that Pol was a close friend of the viscountess, who had asked him to operate her theater in her absence. The whereabouts of the lady remained uncertain in the public's mind.

Actual permission for the opening came from Prince Gawis, who was acting in the name of the king in Celatas.

Ysena spoke again. "I think it is very — vigorous," was her opinion. "Very passionate." The noblewoman looked directly at the young playwright for a moment, before dropping her eyes.

Pol hoped her husband was not paying attention. But he only

allowed the baroness to drag him to these salons so he might drink the prince's wine.

The other guests were already turning their attention to that wine and to the buffet the servants had quietly laid out while he read. Sir Pol smiled. No more should be expected of these nobles.

He would put more trust in the actors back at his theater. Lady Fachalana's theater, that is. Pol wondered what she and Maresta might think of his effort. He had Maresta in mind when he wrote the part of his leading lady.

He'd best find a plate before these highborn freeloaders ate everything.

4

"Can you then do all your father does?"

Fachalalana shook her head. "No more than one could duel a master having read a book on fencing. It would take much practice and great dedication." Leave it to Lomela to ask so practical a question, she thought.

Princess Lomela knew her friend was capable of the passion necessary to master any craft. Would she throw herself into the practice of magic or only dabble?

They were referring to the subject only obliquely, as the seamstress was there, making final adjustments to Lady Fachalana's dress. Nothing in Lomela's wardrobe — nor that of any other woman in the keep — had come close to fitting the noblewoman's lanky frame so a gown must be made up new.

"Where is Maresta this morning?" Again, the presence of the dressmaker meant she must use Ansa's pseudonym.

"Riding," replied Fachalana. "I did not know how much she likes to be on the back of a horse when we were still in Celatas."

"With Sir Blen?"

"Not today. Jobo came up. I do suspect that Guesare will join them outside the walls."

"They not only ride but plot," said Lomela. Fachalana knew that was true.

"We can do our own plotting here," she said, "and on more interesting topics. Do you think Blen likes Maresta?"

An unusual question for her friend, thought Lomela. "Likes her, yes. More than that? Who can tell with Blen. He is a book kept carefully closed." The princess did not add her suspicions as to whom she thought Sir Blen might more than like, even if the man did not admit it to himself.

"I think they would make a good couple," averred Fachalana. "Careful with those pins, Mistress!"

"Sorry, my lady," the woman murmured. She had been paying too much attention to their gossip.

"I like that color on you," the princess said. "Few can properly pull off red."

"Thank you, Lomela. I am partial to it. And know," she added with the smallest of smiles, a smile that seemed to mask an underlying sadness, "that I shall never take to wearing black."

~ ~ ~

The pair looked over the pile of stone before them, a somewhat squat, crumbling tower. From the Anian's spy-friendly house, which was, in fact, a small inn on the roadside, they had traveled south and somewhat westward to reach this spot.

"A minor sorcerer, Sabatare, dwelt here," said Oder. "You would not know him but he was involved in the attack on your uncle's keep."

"Where is he now?" asked Donzalo. It seemed that the wizard was no longer in residence.

"He was among the dead that day."

The Laman knight nodded. "There have been men here not too long ago." The littered courtyard gave evidence of that.

"I believe Lord Radal was staying here with only a small guard. Had we arrived a few days earlier, you and I might have been able to put an end to all of this." Oder obviously regretted the missed opportunity.

Slay Radal? Yes, he and the Anian might well have been able to turn the tables on the sorcerer and accomplish that. Donzalo spoke. "So where has the man gone?" His hand went to the silver wolf, pinned at his shoulder, and his thoughts to when he had last seen the sorcerer, while he had lain dreaming in Fairie.

"Who knows? It seems that he and a large company of men rode out." Oder pointed to tracks leading westward. "All we can do is follow. Let us rest ourselves and our horses here for the night."

"If we pass near the estate of Sir Paren, I would wish to visit."

"As you see fit, Sir Donzalo."

111

THE HAND OF THE SORCERER

~ ~ ~

Ansa was not dissimilar to Dame Tiana in size, albeit somewhat more slender, and wore one of her altered dresses. Tiana had owned only one old gown when she arrived at Castle Rosam but had quickly remedied that. She had to dress her part as wife of the master of arms, after all.

Of course, all those gowns would need altering as Tiana grew more obviously pregnant but that showed little at this time.

While Fachalana lingered in their room that morning, Ansa had attended the religious rite, mostly from curiosity. It somewhat bored her but, as a member of the party that returned from the stoa, she had also partaken of a sumptuous late breakfast. Her comrade had missed out on this reward for virtue, even were it sham virtue.

The Sharshite diplomats showed up in the late afternoon, Lord Doufan and his two right-hand men. Or perhaps we could say that Blen was his left-hand man. Jobareth bore a letter for the Lady Fachalana.

"It's from Modareth!" she told Ansa, breaking the seal. "Lady Carrana is doing well and so is her pregnancy." She looked up. "What would she be, around six months?" Ansa nodded. That should be about right. "Oh, he has had our friend Pol open the theater in our absence. I am not sure how I feel about that!"

"Perhaps better than letting it sit empty."

"Maybe. Pol has also turned to playwriting. You have a rival, Jobo."

Jobareth seemed skeptical. "He's only a boy."

"No younger than our friend Donzalo," Ansa pointed out.

Fachalana smiled at the exchange. "I think Pol has a bit of a crush on you."

"I know he does," replied Ansa. "And I think he is also the sort to get over it without too much difficulty."

"Shall we go down to the hall, my ladies?" asked Blen, who had kept himself out of their conversation. "Allow me to be your escort, " he said, linking his arm with Lady Fachalana's. He had practiced this courtly move carefully.

An amused Jobareth and Ansa followed.

The ball was no great affair but it gave the chance for the wealthy families of Ros-town to mingle with the minor nobility of castle and countryside in a formal setting. Count Borrago had deemed that a good thing and Bolos saw no reason to change it.

Moreover, it gave them all a chance to attempt the latest dances from Sharsh. But, inevitably, the old traditional rounds and reels would prove the most popular. Some of these were similar to those Sir Blen had known as a boy, so he cautiously took part.

Lord Doufan, to the surprise of none who knew him, danced well with many women and charmed all. Months later, people still spoke of his turn with the Lady Lomela, she in a swirl of green satin, he wearing a tunic of deepest blue, in the calf-length cut recently become popular. But they might not have remembered his face.

"You are sitting this one out, my boy?" he asked Blen, who sipped wine punch at one of the tables that had been pushed against the wall to make room for dancing. Blen had doubts as to whether peaches should be added to a proper wine but the taste was not unpleasant.

"It is one of the new dances, sir. I do not know it."

"The ladies would gladly teach you," replied the ambassador. "I have given thought to their request to travel up to the keep of Sir Paren. Count Bolos," he nodded toward the man, stiffly going through the unfamiliar moves, "has no objections, though he can not imagine why they should wish to make such a journey. Moreover, one of his regular patrols of the Abam Road will leave in two days and he suggests they journey with them. So I do not object either." He looked out across the room. "Sir Sorsen seems to be enjoying himself. I assume he too will leave soon."

"Yes, my lord. Both our companies will move south in a few days. I could not say how far south, at this time, for the situation here continues to worry the both of us."

"As it does me." Doufan bowed to a passing woman and continued. "We still have troops across the river."

"In the lands of Count Dordos, yes. I do not know their orders."

"They will come if you or I call for them. Let us hope that does not become necessary."

Music started up, a lively tune led by the shawm. "You would know this dance," said Lord Doufan. "Don't leave all the ladies to me and Sorsen!"

~ ~ ~

"When we sleep, the walls between the worlds grow thin," the chaplain told Princess Mara. "We may glimpse things that are not of this earthly realm."

"Could Kamat send dreams?"

"All things come from Kamat, my daughter," responded the elderly priest. Having given the orthodox answer, he continued. "But there are those who can influence our dreamings. Demons. Powerful sorcerers. Do not put too much trust in those things you may dream."

Mara frowned. "But they can be true, can they not?" she asked.

"They tell more truth about our own minds than aught else. Worry and concern are likely the soil from which your dream grew." The old man took her hand into his own, his soft, dark fingers gently holding hers.

How long since he has used any tool more demanding than a pen? wondered Mara, her mind momentarily wandering from their discussion.

"Mara, I have served you since we left our home and I shall probably die in this foreign land. Know that I shall always watch over you and, with the help of Kamat, try to keep you safe. If there are more such dreams, come to me." The chaplain blessed her and made the sign of the arrow, which the princess dutifully returned.

The priest sat a while in the palace gardens, after the princess had left him. He loved the gardens, the flowers that reminded him of his far away land of birth. Had another touched her dreams? he wondered. Though he had long ago chosen to follow the ways of light, the priest knew something of magic. That was one reason he had been chosen to accompany Mara when she came to wed the crown prince of Sharsh.

And he had felt the disturbances of late, some of which he was certain originated from his own homeland. For Partanaca, now, he felt no loyalty; he served Kamat and Princess Mara, and would remain vigilant in that service.

5

The end of the market season in County Rosam came, more or less, with Autumn Feast. Trade would most certainly continue through the colder months — which were not so cold in this part of Lama — but diminish now along the Great Road and on the River Weldar.

Merchants and traders were winding their ways toward whatever winter quarters they preferred. Some would continue to ply their trade in the south, in Morparas and along the coast of the Minor Sea. Others had homes to which they might return, up and down and across the Weldar's great valley.

Sir Sorsen and his troop were also ready to depart, as was the mixed force of Sharshites and the men of Count Mussago that Blen had commanded. Only one tent remained unstruck at their camp. Within that tent, Sir Blen, Mussago the Younger, and Sorsen held their council.

"I would feel better about this were you accompanying us, Sir Blen," spoke Sorsen. "No offense intended to you or your leadership, Master Mussago," he added, bowing to that taciturn gentleman.

"None is taken. Leading soldiers is not my vocation."

Blen and Sorsen exchanged a quick glance. They knew that Mussago had the admiration and complete loyalty of his men, thanks to his fairness and willingness to work hard alongside them.

Moreover, he was as fine a horseman as either had ever seen. If Mussago did not so disdain knighthood he would long since have had his spurs.

"It seems you must need lead soldiers for a while, my friend," said Sir Blen. "I would not place my second in authority over you."

"I shall be losing my second for a time," spoke Sorsen.

"What? Is Sir Habidros not returning with you?"

"I have given him leave to accompany his friends to the keep of Sir Paren. It was agreeable to me," Orgelo's heir explained, "as I thought it might be wise to have eyes there."

Blen nodded in agreement. "Wise, indeed. That's it then. I'll stay here and you two ride slowly to the south, ready to return if need arises. Let's drink to that and be on our ways." He raised his goblet, drained it, and stepped out into a mild autumn day.

In a few weeks he expected to ride south and rejoin this company, perhaps bringing Habidros with him. After that, who could know?

~ ~ ~

All around the perimeter of the embassy's low-pitched slate roof ran a narrow walkway, shielded by a crenelated wall. Jobareth Nafal peered out over that wall toward the Ros-town road, watching an approaching horseman.

Habidros. Now we can begin our journey, he thought. Jobareth looked down toward the great double stairway that led to the building's main entrance. Its construction should be finished by the time he returned and all that temporary wooden structure would be gone. The embassy would look the way he and Blen had intended, its front dominated by a stone arch that opened into the ground floor with stairs rising on either side to the second story.

Nafal would have no secretary on this trip. He had not taken on a new man since the death of the traitor, Benawis, writing his own dispatches and orders or depending on the fellow who served as Sir Blen's aide — a soldier, but capable enough with a pen. Someone in Sharsh would eventually think to send out a young diplomat to assist him.

Perhaps he could prevail upon Grippo to serve as his secretary while he was at Paren's keep. If possible, he would ask him to come back to the embassy and serve in a more permanent position. The acolyte was being wasted where he was. Grippo could never be officially named as his secretary but there were many other capacities in which he might be useful.

There was Guesare, greeting his brother. He had best go down to his chambers and prepare to ride.

Jobareth turned toward the roof, where rose Sir Blen's false chimney. The legate had examined it on learning of this not-quite-secret way into the embassy. The shaft was topped by a simple trap door, though equipped with a sturdy lock. Blen had presented him with a key. So far as he knew, only the pair and the ambassador held keys.

However, from the inside it was possible to open the hatch without a key. This made sense; the purpose of the lock was to keep intruders out of the embassy, not to prevent the use of the shaft as an escape route. The idea of descending into that dark hole, clinging to a vertical ladder, did not appeal to Jobareth at all, so he did not attempt it.

The stairs were a much better way. Jobareth Nafal opened a door inset into the roof — also requiring one of a restricted number of keys — and started down.

~ ~ ~

"Two men will suffice. Hold the rest here until I send word."

Dovolo nodded. "Yes, my lord. I have chosen a pair to accompany you." He gestured toward a couple of ruffians squatting by their horses. They looked to be casting dice.

"I shall send one back to you when I arrive at Keep Rosam. Start the men moving then. But," Radal continued, "if the second does not meet you with instructions before you reach me, it means that my plan has failed. Disband then and go your way, Sergeant."

My plan must not fail, the sorcerer told himself. For the sake of my king, for the sake of my daughter, I will succeed. Speaking no more, he mounted his steed and rode from camp.

His two attendants scrambled onto their horses, hastening to follow.

"Good luck to you, old man," Dovolo muttered. He turned to his second. "Get these sons of Asak on their feet. We're going to drill every day until our master calls for us."

~ ~ ~

"I think, Dame Tiana, that your husband does not much like me."

Tiana glanced toward Traspa, to see if aught might be read there, before answering. "Sir Jak, he does not like having a force of men in this keep who do not answer to him. When Bolos became count, his personal guard became redundant." That's a good word, thought Tiana. She had never had the opportunity to use such back at Paren's keep. Settling into a chair opposite her guests, she asked, "More tea, Mistress Traspa?"

Traspa held out her cup, once again wishing that Lamans would more frequently choose to offer their guests wine. She noted that Tiana both served and drank with her left hand. Left-handedness was discouraged back in Sharsh as being unlucky, but there seemed to be no stigma to it in this land.

Tiana smiled at the soldier. "I suspect you like to occasionally flaunt your status too."

Mistress Traspa laughed aloud. "Jak likes to do things the way he always has and does not take kindly to suggestions otherwise. That will change," she said with a wink to Tiana, "once we are married."

Sir Jak chose to remain silent on that subject. He looked about the room. These used to be the quarters of Bolos, who had chosen to live separately from his wife. And still did, for that matter, though he had taken a larger suite since becoming count. They had changed, that was certain — there was nothing left of Count Bolos in this room. Would Traspa change his quarters? Would she change him?

Which made him think of something else. "Traspa, where are we going to live? Not in one of our little rooms, surely?" he asked, not so surely.

"There are several unoccupied rooms available," Tiana told them. As wife of the master of arms, she had taken upon herself the duty of assigning quarters. No one had asked her to so do, but Dame Tiana did not mind that. "Donzalo's old chambers are still empty. Both of them."

"One is too grand," opined Traspa, "and the other is a dungeon." Jak nodded in agreement to her assessment.

"For your honeymoon, at least," Tiana said, the idea having just come to her, "you might use Copago's cottage. No one has resided there since his family left. And," she added, "I might just be able to convince my husband that it should be yours permanently." Actually, she thought, he would welcome the opportunity to have Jak outside the walls.

And Bolos would would not at all mind giving such a wedding gift to his most trusted man. Especially in that it would cost him nothing.

Traspa and Jak looked at each other. It was obvious that they liked the idea.

"So," continued Dame Tiana, "now that the festival is past and most of our guests have departed, we could have a wedding anytime." She raised an eyebrow and looked expectantly upon the couple.

"I'd do it right now if a priest were here," avowed Sir Jak. Mistress Traspa did not seem to have any objections to the idea.

"I think Countess Lomela will want a day or two of warning," laughed Tiana. "You are very important to her, Traspa." She turned to the knight. "As you are to the count, sir. I think he cares about you deeply, in his way.

"What say you to three days from now?" That would give her plenty of time to set things up. Tiana relished the thought of being able to take charge of such an event. She would prove that she had a role to play in Castle Rosam.

"Three days," agreed Traspa, and kissed her husband-to-be.

~ ~ ~

"I hope you do not mind traveling quickly," said the captain. He turned his eyes toward the Lady Fachalana, who did not appear well this morning, slumping wearily in the saddle. Fachalana did have her own horse back now, a tall bay stallion from Sharsh, and was choosing to sit astraddle, as she had on her journey into Lama.

Jobareth answered. His rank and gender marked him as apparent leader of the little group of travelers. He doubted that he could actually assert any sort of authority over any of them. "The sooner we arrive, sir, the better. We know that the patrols do not dawdle on their way."

The company was mixed. The ambassador had insisted that a pair of embassy guards be added to the party. Nafal felt it not a bad idea

— who could know what might be needed once they parted ways with the count's men? These two men at arms and the five travelers, with the patrol of ten men and their captain, brought them to eighteen.

There were also several pack-horses, including a pair laden with the ladies' luggage.

"Then, sir, if we do not have to turn aside for any reason, we should have you all at Sir Paren's manor in three days. There is always the possibility that we will have to chase after outlaws or help a traveler in need or any of a dozen other things that may happen on the road." The captain smiled and attempted a nonchalant shrug. It did not suit him. "You would then have to wait on us. The count does not want you traveling on your own."

"Nor would we wish to," replied the legate. A sound, serious fellow, he thought. He knew the soldier had a good reputation.

Jobareth turned to his friends. "Are we ready?"

"An hour ago," said Guesare. "I would have been prepared even sooner if I hadn't need wait on this malingerer." He nodded toward his brother.

"I've more important things to do all day than strum a rebec," responded Habidros.

"Aye, get in an extra hour of sleep."

"'Twill make me fresher for the road," came the answer and both laughed.

The captain nodded. "Take a place behind my lead four," he ordered and wordlessly signaled for his men to ride.

It was a pleasant, cool day and Fachalana soon roused herself enough to converse gaily as they rode along. But by afternoon, she seemed worn and more so the following day.

6

"My brother seems to be enjoying your farce," said Modareth, looking toward the crown prince's box. "The Princess Mara too."

Pol nodded, somewhat absentmindedly. His attention was on the stage. "I had truly intended to present something from repertoire but this came rushing out."

A portly figure with preposterous mustachios strode onto the stage and bellowed out a song. On the balcony above him, an exaggeratedly homely maiden — obviously played by a middle-aged man — pantomimed her passion with the broadest of histrionics.

"I can think of more than one of our friends who might be the inspiration for this Baron Bumbiap," the prince whispered to his wife.

"And the two young female leads are obviously drawn from Fachalana and Maresta," came her reply. She glanced toward their youthful playwright. "Pol may need to be more cautious with his lampooning."

"Hmm, yes." It was like the impractical Modareth to not think of such things. As a prince of the realm, it was not something he would ever have need considered anyway. "I think 'Bumbiap' is a success," he spoke more loudly. "My congratulations to you, Sir Pol."

"Thank you, sir. If you will excuse me, I must be back to my players." Pol bowed toward Princess Carrana. "My lady." He turned and hurried from their box.

"I think it a success, too," said Carrana.

Prince Modareth looked again toward his older brother's box, directly across the hall, and remembered something. "Mara is with child," he announced.

"Hush, there is a song coming." They had, of course, heard the entire play read to them by young Pol so they knew what was next. The youthful hero of the comedy stepped forward.

I've given you my heart
to do with as you please,
to break beneath your heel
or heal its injuries.
And nothing more I'll ask
of you, no words save these:
remember how my love
came singing on the breeze.

Oft wounded in the past,
I'll not avoid love's dart
nor falter on a journey
I once feared to start.
This starry, vernal night,
though we be far apart,
remember how my love
came singing from the heart.

As the applause faded, Princess Carrana turned to her husband. "Mara is pregnant? Where did you hear that?"

"The most reliable of sources," Modareth replied with a grin. "My brother."

"That must please Gawis. I did not know he and his wife were still intimate."

"They seem to have grown closer, lately. Perhaps we have set them a good example." The prince winked at his wife. "Gawis will be more pleased if it turns out to be a boy."

"And maybe the threats against your life will be over."

"I fear they will never be over, wife. It is the fate of princes." He did not add, 'and of their wives.' But both thought it.

~ ~ ~

"It would be best, perhaps, if I did not come to your uncle's keep."

"You have nothing to fear from Sir Paren," responded Donzalo.

Oder shrugged. "Maybe so. I should make contact with our friend

Guesare. Where he is right now, I do not know, but Ros-town would be a good place to start."

"Then travel from Paren's keep. It is less than three days hard ride from town and there might be news awaiting us."

"Very well. I must have a different name when we arrive. Tell all that I am a minstrel friend of Guesare." The Anian frowned in thought for a moment. "I shall be a Cuddonian. Call me Remare."

One who follows Rema, the earth goddess, thought Donzalo. Guesare's patroness. He smiled at the little jest in Oder's choice. "Then, Sir Remare, let us cross the river as did those before us."

Their tracking had brought them to this spot where Radal's men had gone over the Abam. In these highlands, the flow was not wide and there were many places it could be forded.

"Your uncle should know about these men," observed Oder. On the north side of the stream, they could see that the tracks led off into the wilderness, rather than turning south toward Paren's manor and Ros-town. "Later, perhaps, we can follow their trail again."

Donzalo nodded soberly. "They are passing far too near his keep. He may want to send out a patrol to investigate."

"'Twould be better than having we two stumble upon them. We'll leave it to Sir Paren." Oder eyed a narrow path to their left. "This, then, is our way. How far, do you reckon? Two days?"

"No more, I would think." The young Laman was not particularly familiar with this area, though he had passed through, going the opposite direction, a year earlier.

He urged his horse forward through an autumn forest of gold and red.

~ ~ ~

So, his old friend was marrying. Perdos considered Jak to be a friend, or, at least, not an enemy.

An enemy — he had only now learned that Guesare was gone, journeying with a group of travelers to the keep of Sir Paren. It would have done him little good to know this earlier, as the minstrel was in the company of soldiers and better protected than when he lingered in Ros-town. Should he follow?

Perhaps later. That company should arrive at their destination this day, the day of Jak's wedding. He had decided to stick around for that. Not that he would have been welcomed as a guest.

No, he would have undoubtedly been arrested on sight. But later, he had heard, the couple would be honeymooning at Copago's old cottage. Maybe he could drop by discreetly in a day or two and offer his congratulations. Jak wouldn't turn him in.

And he might have useful news.

Ah, this must be they leaving the castle. Perdos stood in his stirrups to get a better look at the wedding party proceeding from the outer gate. He dared not come any closer

Even the count was there. Bolos could be a good sort, he remembered. He always did right by me, Perdos told himself. Better than I did by him.

There were the newlyweds heading up the road in a flower-festooned donkey cart. The wedding party was dispersing and Perdos had best be on his way too. It would not do to lurk near the gates of Keep Rosam over long.

It was good that Jak had found someone. A good woman, too, this Traspa, as he recalled. The knight, perhaps, felt a moment of envy, a touch, even, of self-pity, before allowing himself a smile and turning his mount toward Ros-town.

~ ~ ~

I should have my father's books, thought Fachalana. There was much in them that might be useful.

Jobareth Nafal looked up from the papers he was holding. "You're awake. Feeling better, my lady?"

She nodded. "Where is Ansa?"

"Out exploring. Our friend is rather taken with this land. I must say, I find it pleasant myself."

There are spells in those books, she told herself. I need to know more. To her companion, she said, "I was very tired, Jobo. How long have I slept?"

"It is near noon now."

Fachalana recalled arriving around dusk. She must have gone to bed immediately but that she did not remember. "I'm hungry!"

"I shall send for something." Jobareth started to rise.

"No, no. I want to get up and get doing. Let me dress and we'll go find some lunch."

The diplomat chuckled. "Your luggage is already unpacked." He waved an arm toward an oaken wardrobe on the other side of the small, stone-walled room. "I'll be outside," he told her and took his leave.

Yes, I need spells, the young woman thought as she quickly slipped into a simple gown, brown with red accents, and suited to almost any occasion. Fachalana knew that the words of a spell had no power of their own. They served only to focus the mind on the task at hand. But focus was what most she required.

There was a young man waiting outside the door with Nafal. It took her a moment to put a name to him.

"Why, Brother Grippo! I almost didn't recognize you without your robes."

"I know not when I shall don those again, my lady." The former acolyte was clad in nondescript tunic and soft boots. "If ever," he added.

"My brother and his family are about to take lunch. Will you join us?"

"Gladly," she replied, taking his arm. Jobareth followed them down the narrow hallway. Fachalana looked about her. "Are we inside the keep?"

"Inside the walls, my lady, but not in the keep proper. This is one of the houses that surround it."

"Paren has chosen to add these rather than build a larger keep," said Jobareth, "as the numbers of those living at the manor have increased."

"Yes. There are more houses outside the walls, as well," Grippo said.

Not well suited for defense, thought Fachalana. It's more like a village than a castle.

The door to Copago's suite stood open. A little girl ran to greet them. "What is her name?" whispered the noblewoman.

"Ramapa," answered Grippo. "It's a Muramized variant of a very old Laman name."

Another scholar, she thought. I can't seem to get away from them. She knelt to say hello to the child. "How do you do, Mistress Ramapa?"

The girl looked to her uncle, who gave her an encouraging smile. "This is the Lady Fachalana, Ramapa."

"Hello, Fasalama." She turned and scurried back to her parents.

"Something smells quite good," said Fachalana, rising to her feet.

"Something always smells good in here," Grippo replied. "The one great advantage of not being made a priest is that I get to eat meat for another year."

"Come on in and have a seat," invited Dame Janona. "There is plenty of stew."

Sir Copago half-rose from his place to acknowledge them and then returned to his bowl. "You might or might not recognize what has gone into the pot," said he. "There is wild meat aplenty about these parts."

"I feel as hungry as a wild beast myself," answered Fachalana, taking a place at the long table. "And I think when I am done I shall have to return to my lair and sleep some more. Yes, Jobareth," she said, seeing the look of concern on his face, "our journey taxed me more than I realized. But I should be fine after a bit more rest."

And certain elixirs she had brought with her. That was all she needed, she was sure.

~ ~ ~

"Something is afoot at Keep Rosam. The count has ordered the gates closed and would not let me enter."

The ambassador sighed. "I regret already letting Nafal leave. Bolos trusts him more than he does either of us."

"His father did," said Sir Blen. "I am not so certain Count Bolos feels the same."

"Perhaps so. Whatever is happening, gossip is bound to reach our ears in time." Lord Doufan turned back to the cleaning of a pair of compact pistols laid out on his desk. Blen did not recall ever seeing the weapons before though he knew the man sometimes carried them concealed. "Keep yours open, Blen."

"Yes, my lord." He hesitated a moment, as though it might be best to leave the conversation there, but then chose to speak on. "The legate and his friends should have arrived at their destination yesterday."

Doufan did not look up from his task. "I have no doubt the Lady Fachalana will grow quickly bored up there in the country. I would expect them to return within the fortnight."

7

Sir Pol's play had been a great success, by all reports. Her husband had laughed uproariously during the performance but Princess Mara could not quite follow it. That was of no importance — she was often baffled by the ways of her adopted homeland.

The handsome young playwright and impresario had taken a bow at the end of the performance. Mara had seen him about the palace on occasion — he was, after all, a protege of her brother-in-law — but this night there had seemed something more familiar about him, as though he were a long-ago acquaintance, half-forgotten. Yet they had never even spoken, to Mara's recollection.

That night she had dreamed. Pol was in her dreams and her husband and they all spoke lines upon a stage. The words made no sense to Mara or, if they did, she forgot them upon awakening.

But she did remember Prince Gawis lying dead at the end of their scene.

Maybe her chaplain was correct. Maybe these dreams were but the result of worry and concern. Mara sighed. She had another concern now, a child on the way. May Kamat give her a son this time!

She would write to Sir Pol, she decided, congratulate him on his success, invite him to one of their parties. That would do no harm and Mara could learn more of the young knight.

Somehow, she felt she should.

~ ~ ~

A woman stepped out into the road, well ahead of them. Blond was her hair and her short gown was of white. A recurved bow hung from her shoulder; a white wolf followed at her heels.

"Diba," whispered Donzalo.

Oder looked sharply toward his companion and then back to the figure. "Nay, friend Donzalo, it is my sister."

"So it is," agreed the young knight, seemingly not the least embarrassed about his mistake. "So it is. Ansa — and that is King with her." He slipped from his saddle and raised a hand in greeting. "Ansa!"

She had looked so alike to the alabaster statue in the shrine of Diba, the site of his Yule Eve vigil less than a year before. That time seemed distant now, like a dream of his childhood. He touched the silver wolf pinned at his shoulder and momentarily lost himself in the memory.

Then he crouched to pet the dog that had come bounding to him.

"Greetings to you, Sir Donzalo," said the Anian girl, leisurely approaching the pair of travelers. "And to you, my brother. Guesare will be pleased to see both of you."

"He is here?" asked Oder, who had dismounted to stand beside Donzalo.

"He is, as is his brother Habidros. At the moment, they are off practicing marksmanship with Sir Guesare's rifle."

"I would assume the Lady Fachalana accompanied you?" said Donzalo.

"Yes, though most would say I accompanied her," Ansa replied. "Jobareth did so, as well. By the way," she continued, "name me Maresta here, not Ansa. Our friends may all know who I am but Sir Paren and his people do not."

Donzalo nodded. "Then, my Lady Maresta, allow me to introduce you to my friend, Sir Remare."

Ansa glanced at her brother and laughed. It was, perhaps, not a musical laugh but it was an honest one and a hearty one. "A Cuddonian, eh? The unshaven pair of you look like you just came down from the hills."

"We did," admitted Oder, rubbing his chin. "But I do not intend to maintain this part of my disguise."

"Come along, then," said Ansa. "We are near the manor."

The two joined her as she started up the trail, one on either side, leading their mounts. Donzalo watched her converse with her brother, catching up on all his news, and noted again how she looked like the goddess Diba. *She is a silver woman, as Jola was golden,* thought he.

Though most of Donzalo's logical mind scoffed at the idea, a part of him, a place deep within his wounded heart, could not help but take it as a sign.

~ ~ ~

This fellow did not know Perdos and neither he nor Jak intended to change that. The sergeant had been calling him Dos, as in the old days, and they left it at that when he joined them.

"There he was at the gate, looking like an old beggar," said the soldier. "We had no idea who he was." He took a quaff of his beer. "Good stuff, Jak."

"Captain Corgos sent a keg down as a wedding present," Jak replied. "I think he would prefer to keep me here drinking it as long as possible. Here," he said, taking the man's tankard, "let me get you a refill. Do you need any, Dos? No?" He went to the barrel and filled his guest's cup, as well as his own.

"The wife is up visiting her princess. You'd think she would be happy to have a few days off but she believes they can't get by without her in the keep. So," said Jak, setting the beer down in front of his visitor, "it was Lord Radal. That was bold of the man."

Having had dealings in the past with Radal, Perdos did not feel overly surprised by such an action. Not that he truly knew the sorcerer — did anyone? — but he had seen enough of his ways.

He looked about the little cottage. This was where Borrago's bastard and his family lived, eh? Good riddance to them — he had never gotten on well with Copago. Perdos had dropped by an hour earlier, to the surprise of his old sergeant, and, with the Dame Traspa absent, the two sat and drank uninterrupted. Until this soldier showed up, bursting with news from the keep.

"The count let him in?" he asked.

"That he did," replied the man. "Had him taken to the tower. He'll keep him there until he decides what to do with him, I reckon."

"I'd send him straight back to his old master," declared Sir Jak. "Maybe minus his head."

131

But he doesn't trust the king of Sharsh, Perdos said to himself. Bolos is mistrustful of everyone these days.

Aloud, he said, "Could be he hopes to bargain with him."

"That's a dangerous game," replied Jak.

His companions nodded their agreement to this and drank of Jak's good beer.

~ ~ ~

"It was the king who was behind all this. I acted only on his orders."

Bolos half-believed the former lord councilor. He had no doubt that Lareth's hand had been in all that had happened. But he was not inclined to see Lord Radal as without guilt.

Sir Corgos remained silent. The count would have appreciated a word of advice now; he had to admit that Copago, as much as he may have disliked the man, would always have had something useful to say.

But he did appreciate his master of arms' solid presence. It was reassuring, as was that of the two guardsmen who accompanied him. Bolos would not have wanted to be alone with this sorcerer.

Why was he here? That was the foremost concern. But another question, one ultimately of more import to Bolos, lay behind it: had Radal been involved in his father's assassination?

He would not ask now but he would have the truth from this man.

"That does not make you blameless, sir," he said to the dark nobleman. "Why should I not send you back to Sharsh in bonds? For that matter, why should I not hang you from my walls?"

"Because I might be useful to you, my lord. Because you are surrounded by enemies who would throw down all you and your forebears have built." The sorcerer sighed. "My own master among them, I fear. I have fallen from favor for opposing him."

Corgos snorted. There was no obvious response from the impassive Radal, yet malice danced in his eyes. This captain could prove a stumbling-block to his plans.

"Hmmph." Bolos pondered a moment, before speaking to his master of arms. "See that he remains in the tower. Guards both above and below this floor." Turning back to the Sharshite, he stared at the man for a long moment. So old, he seemed, so frail. Yet dangerous, he was certain. Then, shaking his head, he left him.

~ ~ ~

At last. Lareth placed the dispatch on his desk and gazed out through the stone archways toward the east. At last, news of Radal.

But in Castle Rosam? That was baffling. It baffled his ambassador there, Lord Doufan, as well, but the man had made a formal complaint to the count, stating that Radal had fled from custody in Sharsh and requesting his return.

That was well. Bolos might even do as asked.

He should write the count himself. Yes, and at the same time, alert all the Sharshite companies in Lama to stand ready. Then, he would have to depend on the steady hands of Doufan and of Sir Blen to act when needed, to keep this from being the match that lit up all of Lama.

For a short while, Lareth listened to the steady beat of the kettle-drums, as his men marched and maneuvered outside the walls of the keep. Those drums were one good thing the Ani had brought with them to Sharsh.

"Take dictation," the king told his secretary, settling back into his chair. "We have much to do."

8

"This dance is so simple even Sir Blen would have no trouble with it."

"Do they ever go in the opposite direction?" asked Fachalana. It seemed that they had been circling to their left forever.

"Never," Jobareth replied, stepping sideways and then following with his right foot to bring his heels together. "This is how the Carole has been danced for centuries, or so Donzalo told me."

"If I knew any of these songs I would attempt to sing along." The Lady Fachalana giggled at a thought. "Were Modi here he would want to write them all down in a book."

Many of the circle of dancers were joining into the singing. Some of the tunes were faster, others slower, and the dancing followed their rhythm and that of an accompanying hand drum with the stamping of feet and the striking together of clogged heels.

"Our Maresta may well be committing them all to memory. Would you like to drop out for a while?"

Fachalana nodded. She looks strong enough today, thought Nafal, but there is no point in tempting things. The two left the circle, which was immediately closed again as the couples on either side linked hands.

"We should mount an entertainment," the noblewoman declared, sipping from a cup of cool cider her companion brought her. "Perhaps a read-through of your play, Jobo."

"I thought you considered it unfinished, my lady."

"It would help you to see its many weaknesses," she told him. Although Fachalana smiled, Jobareth Nafal knew she very much meant it. "You and I and Ansa and — who else? We should have another reader or two."

"Grippo, maybe? He is well lettered. In fact," he confided, "I have prevailed upon him to come back to Ros-town with me and serve as my secretary for a time."

"Yes, he would do. As actor, I mean. I've no idea how good a secretary he might be. I wonder if Remare can act." Though she knew the man as Ansa's brother, Fachalana would not reveal that identity.

Jobareth himself had recognized who the man truly was, but likewise chose to speak not of it. "Guesare's friend?" asked he. "I know not. He has not drawn much attention to himself since arriving. Now what is this?"

A messenger had discreetly entered the courtyard and handed a dispatch to Sir Paren, who gave it a quick perusal and then beckoned his nephew and his master of arms to join him. Following a moment's whispering, he waved Jobareth to him, as well.

Whether the reeve meant to include her or not, Fachalana decided to include herself.

"It is your father, my lady," Donzalo said to her. "He is in Castle Rosam." He turned to the legate. "We must leave at once!"

~ ~ ~

"Someone is in a great hurry behind us," remarked Master Mussago.

Sorsen held up a gauntleted hand, signaling their troop to halt. "Let's see who it is."

They sat their horses, watching the figure draw closer. The day was damp and cool, and a mist lay upon the road so they could not make out a face till the rider was nearly upon them.

"Why, 'tis Sir Blen!" exclaimed Sorsen. "I did not expect him so soon."

"Trouble, no doubt," opined his companion.

"No doubt," agreed the knight. "Or news, at least. We'll know soon."

"If it's important enough to ride after us, then it will take some time." Mussago stood in his stirrups and called to the men. "Make camp here.

"I'm going to get down and stretch my legs," he informed Sorsen.

For a moment, the son of Orgelo was annoyed that his ostensible second-in-command was issuing orders, but then he shrugged. "Good idea," he said, and dismounted as well.

Shortly, Blen was down from his mount and greeting the pair. "The news is straightforward enough," he told them. "Lord Radal is at Keep Rosam. We suspect his men are nearby."

Mussago spat. "We go back then?"

"No," replied Sir Sorsen. "Best to wait on developments and be ready."

"You two have the authority of your fathers to back you up," Blen said. "One of these minor counts should be willing to let you linger near the Rosam borders."

"Poised to return if needed." Sorsen turned to his fellow nobleman. "We should send swift couriers to both our sires with this news."

"Aye." The lean Laman sighed. "I hope something happens soon, one way or another. I would hate to miss being home for Harvest Feast."

~ ~ ~

Perdos did not care over much about the intrigues of Lord Radal and his presence at Castle Rosam, but did recognize that they would inevitably impact his own business. This, he thought, should send Guesare and his friends scurrying back.

He felt safer loitering about Ros-town these days. His banishment was old and forgotten news; no one paid attention to him, all too caught up in the goings-on at the keep. Wild rumors spread among the dock workers and the tradesmen who frequented these taverns. He listened to much but believed little.

An elderly man settled into the place opposite him. Perdos looked him up and down. A fighting man, once, he surmised, and of no importance to him. He turned his attention back to the plate of sausages and corn cakes before him.

"Sir Perdos, I assume?"

"How do you know me, sir?" His left hand sought the knife in his boot, even as he asked.

The old fellow chuckled. "There are many voices that whisper in my ear. One told me of an outlawed knight who lurked in Ros-town, waiting on his chance for vengeance."

He leaned forward and spoke more lowly. "I am Lord Doufan, but you may address me here as Old Dog. We might be of assistance to each other." He held up a hand to attract a passing serving-wench. "Bring us a couple beers, my dear."

Perdos again eyed the nondescript man before him. Doufan, eh? Not really so old, either. "Speak, Old Dog."

"I have heard of your recent exploits in Todmouth. You did the world a great favor there and crippled Radal in the process. That I personally appreciate."

"Radal is none of my concern and I care not one way nor the other for your appreciation." He drank deeply from his tankard. "But I do thank you for the beer."

"I can provide more than beer. Gold, for one thing.

"But you want the Cuddonian minstrel. I am aware of that." The Sharshite spoke as though he were confiding in an old friend. "I know Guesare and I like him. But he is a spy for the Ani and, therefor, not to be entirely trusted. Ah, you didn't know that, did you?"

"I did not. But I can't say I am surprised."

"It may or may not be to my advantage — Sharsh's advantage — if he lives. You might say I am neutral on the issue."

Perdos slowly nodded. This he understood. But to what was all of it leading?

"What I do need is another set of eyes, one known only to me and reporting only to me. You know the keep and many of the men there. That is useful.

"I can give you official papers, identifying you as attached to the embassy. You will be able to come and go more freely. Of course, someone might still recognize you but you have seemed willing to chance that. How are those sausages, by the way? I'm feeling a mite hungry."

"Middling," replied Sir Perdos. "They spice everything too heavily down here in the south."

"That they do," agreed the ambassador. "Think on my offer, sir. And if you think to accept it, meet me here tomorrow." He rose and left, but not without placing silver on the table that would more than cover both their tabs.

A sly old fox, thought Perdos, his naturally distrustful nature taking over. Still, a bit of money and a chance to get close to the minstrel was tempting. He would indeed think about it.

~ ~ ~

"It is much easier to be someone else when one has a well-written script, my lord."

Modareth nodded slowly. "I have enough trouble, Pol, remembering my own story, much less that of someone else."

"Then perhaps, sir, I should say it is also easier to be ones own self when properly prepared."

The prince smiled. "Maybe so!" He lifted his reading glass, the lens that ever dangled from a bit of black ribbon about his neck, to his eye and peered at the bottle he held. "Clever idea, putting wine into glass containers like this."

"Your brother has had a part in that. Prince Gawis has done much to foster the glass industry here in Celatas."

"And now he wishes to show off his success. Here he comes," he said. The crown prince approached slowly, acknowledging his guests as he crossed the crowded room.

On reaching them, he nodded casually to Pol, who bowed gracefully, and took Modareth's hand. "I see, my brother, that you have been examining the wine bottles," said he, attempting not to sound too obviously proud. "Only a few years ago we could not have produced glass strong enough for this."

"The coals of the earth permit this, do they not, your highness?"

"Indeed they do, Sir Pol, with the great heat of their fires," he answered, slightly raising an eyebrow in momentary surprise at the question, before resuming a proper princely demeanor. This young fellow is a bright one, isn't he? he asked himself. He must tell Mara to invite him again.

Gawis then looked his younger brother up and down. "Are these to be your colors?"

Modareth blushed and stammered out, "Ca — Carrana thought I should have my own." Then he laughed. "But I did not let her choose them!"

"No green," stated Prince Gawis. "I can understand that." Green was not only associated with the king and, now, himself, but also with Partanaca. After the recent assassination attempts, Modareth would naturally be sour on the color.

"Your argent and purple are the colors of Dor," he continued. "You no doubt intended that." And, therefor, also the colors of our grandfather, he noted to himself. "It would seem you have heard that Father intends to name you Duke of Dor." How did Modareth learn what they thought a well-kept secret? His brother was showing unexpected capabilities and the man at his side might have something to do with that.

Modareth sighed. "Am I to be stuck there, administering provincial bureaucrats?"

"Such duties attend your birth, my lord," Pol remarked. "The freest men are neither slaves nor kings."

"Ah, a proverb! You sound like Lord Doufan," laughed Prince Gawis.

"I consider that high praise, your highness," replied the young knight, with a bow.

He bowed as well to Princess Mara, who had come to stand wordlessly beside her husband. "My lady," murmured Pol and kissed the hand she extended.

"Mara, how are you?" asked Modareth, taking that hand into his own. "We see too little of you." His Carrana had frequently extended invitations to their sister-in-law, invitations that were politely declined. The shy prince, perhaps more than anyone else in their circle, could understand this.

"I do well, Modareth," she replied. "And now we do see each other, no?"

"Indeed, my lady, we come to you." Did that sound wrong? Modareth did not want it to seem he was chiding her. He looked about the room. Where had his wife gotten to? She was better at this sort of thing.

Recognizing his patron's discomfort, Pol intervened. "I think, sir, I would come as often as possible."

"You are always welcome, Sir Pol," said Gawis, "with or without my brother." He winked at Modareth. "We greatly enjoyed our evening at your theater."

"It remains the theater of the Viscountess Fachalana, your highness. I but mind the place till the lady returns. I am gladdened that you enjoyed our performance and I thank you for kind words — and for your invitation."

"We thank you, Sir Pol," Mara said. "I have not seen my husband laugh so in years." She went on, somewhat sheepishly. "But you must explain to me sometime what all of it meant. I fear there was much I did not understand!"

"With pleasure, my lady. But in return, you must play upon the dulcimer for us. Prince Modareth has spoken highly of your skill."

Said prince reddened. Perhaps Mara did as well, beneath the darkness of her countenance.

"She would be pleased to so do," averred Prince Gawis. "I have not heard you play in far too long a time, my dear," he said, turning to his wife.

The princess smiled. "Then, Husband, you should sit in on our daughters' lessons."

As the group chuckled over that, Mara took the opportunity to look more closely at the young playwright. Yes, he did seem so familiar and she thought now she knew why.

Could it be that Sir Pol was the man she had seen in her dreams?

~ ~ ~

"May Kamat be with you. I shall follow as soon as I may, with the ladies and Sir Habidros."

"Will it be safe for you, sir, and for your people here?" asked Guesare. "There is still an armed company somewhere in the wilds."

"My scouts have only now reported signs of Radal's men, moving southward toward Castle Rosam. It would seem," said Sir Paren, "that they have no interest in my keep. Sir Copago and a troop rides to follow them."

"Then let us ride too," spoke Donzalo, impatient with any delay. "It is time to bring all this to a close."

"That it is," Oder asserted firmly. Though he had remained quiet and unassuming throughout his stay, Paren had sensed that the supposed minstrel was a man used to issuing orders — and to having them followed.

"Legate," said he, holding up a packet to Jobareth. "I have written to your ambassador. Make certain Doufan receives these, will you? And he may share them with you should he choose."

Nafal took the papers, nodded his assent, and spurred his mount to catch up with his comrades, already riding ahead. The two Sharshite guardsmen who had accompanied him from the embassy fell in behind.

9

"Openly camp and offer no harm, he said."

Dovolo nodded. "And that is all?"

"Once you're settled, he wants you to go to the castle, alone. Let 'em know you're friendly." The soldier frowned into space, as if trying to remember if there was anything more. "They watched us when they let me in to talk, so they'll be expecting you, I reckon. If he can, the boss will get word to you one way or another about what's next."

"Refer to our master as Lord Radal," came Dovolo's curt reply. He *would* maintain discipline among this lot.

"Right, Sergeant. Sorry."

Dovolo nodded. "Good. Go get yourself some grub." He turned from the man in dismissal.

So he was supposed to go marching into Keep Rosam, eh? Well, if the old man could do it, so could he.

And this spot, a clearing in the woods no more than a half-day's ride from the castle, would do as their camp. Best he get the men organized and then follow Radal's orders. Whatever the consequences.

~ ~ ~

"I know you still seek the life of Donzalo. And I know why."

"And I know your secret," came Radal's reply.

Lomela shrugged. "It would do you no good to speak of it."

"Probably not." So like her father, he thought, more so than either of his sons. "Let us, then, speak of other things.

"You have seen my daughter recently. Is she well, my lady?"

The princess hesitated. "She — seems tired, sir." Her tone became accusatory. "That, I think, is in part your doing."

"Her doing, as well," sighed the nobleman. "She is at the embassy?"

"I think that knowledge is for Fachalana to divulge."

"But she will not speak to me, though she knows there is no

longer any reason to fear revealing herself. I can see nothing of her mind. Neither can she see mine."

"What she fears, my lord, is the pain of such a conversation."

Radal went to the narrow window and peered out across the Castle Rosam's courtyard, where lay the long deep shadows of the battlements. It was nearing evening and would soon be dark. Yes, everything would soon be dark.

"Even your own shadow leaves you when you are in darkness," the sorcerer said, almost whispering, before turning back to Lomela. "Perhaps you should leave now as well, my lady."

"As you wish, Lord Radal."

Followed by one of the count's personal guardsmen who had waited outside the door, Lady Lomela descended the narrow curving way to the room where her husband and Sir Corgos sat. This had once been Borrago's office; now, the master of arms occupied it. The guard took up a post at the foot of the stairs.

"Could you find out what the man wants?" asked Count Bolos.

"He wants your brother's life. That I could have told you without speaking to him." The princess sat herself down on one of the hard chairs. Was that wine on the table? She could use some. No, just her husband's barley-water. "And you knew it already, did you not?"

"But why?" Bolos wondered. "Why does he so hate the lad?" He was clearly exasperated by all that was going on about him. "Ah, well, Donzalo is safely come to our uncle's manor, according to the latest word from Sir Paren. Best he stays there."

Lomela and Corgos exchanged a look before the captain spoke. "I fear, my lord, that he will not."

~ ~ ~

Mussago and Sorsen could manage matters without him. They were capable men. It was best that Blen return as quickly as possible to County Rosam.

It was likely that Jobareth would be returning too. Word would have reached Sir Paren's keep by now.

As for the others who had journeyed there, who could say? It might be best were the women to remain safely distant from Rostown but Blen doubted greatly that they would. Certainly not the headstrong Fachalana. She would not let herself be pushed to the side.

And Radal was her father. He had to keep that in mind.

The knight had never known anyone like the Lady Fachalana. He could picture her in his mind, remembering her as he had faced her in their fencing. Could one want for a better woman by ones side? But she was promised to Nafal, after all, and he himself was only a knight of no particular importance, a younger son of a minor baronet.

It had been nearly a decade since he had run away from his father's modest estate by the River Chas, yet it sometimes seemed no more than yesterday. He wondered if the salmon yet swam in the shadows of the willow-lined river banks. Of course they do, he told himself. They are not the ones who left.

So mused Sir Blen as he hurried north along the Great Road.

~ ~ ~

It was the company whose deserted camp he had come across south of the Abam. Of this Perdos was sure. There were not as many as had once followed the late Sojel, but they were undoubtedly the same men. The men who had murdered his friends.

This he did not say to Lord Doufan. He had taken the ambassador's papers and, aye, his gold as well. The man had asked the knight to first undertake this task for him, to scout out the disposition of Radal's troop.

"It was easy enough. There was a hill that gave me a clear vantage of the area. If that rabble had been any sort of soldiers, they would have had their own sentry up there." Perdos took a swig from his cup. Real perry like they made in the north — he hadn't had any in ages.

Another man might have guessed that the Sharshite had known this and ordered a keg. Perdos chose to enjoy the drink rather than question it.

"I was about to head back when I saw movement in the woods near the camp. Up high like I was I could tell it was a troop of soldiers and they meant those fellows no good.

"They must have tracked them from the east. I could see their captain had his riders stationed to charge the camp. Radal's men would have been slaughtered."

"And were they?" asked Doufan, as nonchalantly as if they were discussing the weeding of a garden.

"No, I'm sorry to say."

The ambassador only nodded and waited for Perdos to continue.

"Well, their leader and a couple men rode into camp, as boldly as you please, to tell them to surrender. I could recognize the fool even at that distance. It was Sir Copago."

"A fool indeed, but very like him not to attack without warning."

"That it is," admitted Sir Perdos. He might dislike the man but he respected him for his uncompromising sense of honor. "Anyway, one of those knaves sauntered right up and held out a piece of paper to him. The captain did not like what he read one bit. Threw it on the ground and wheeled his mount around."

Lord Doufan frowned. "I would hazard that the count had given them his permission to be there. What did our Copago then?"

"He led his men straight up the hill where I was watching, so I hurried away. If I were he, I'd be camped up there watching that bunch."

"As would I." Doufan looked out toward the river. There was little traffic, late on this autumn day. "I think we may leave them to Sir Copago for now. As for you, I have no assignment other than to keep your eyes open. Meet me here the day after tomorrow. You may," he continued, "sleep here if you wish. Those who abide in this house are discreet."

They were seated in a low ramshackle edifice near the mouth of the Abam, set on piles driven into the marshy ground.

"I think I prefer my bed on higher ground, sir," replied Perdos, "and in air less soggy."

145

"And in some spot unknown to me, as well," said Doufan.

"Aye, that too," agreed Perdos, emptying his cup.

~ ~ ~

"I intend to let you and your wife have that cottage as your own, once this trouble has passed, but for now I want you here in the keep."

"Thank you, sir," replied Jak. "We had honeymoon enough. I'm ready to serve."

As dependable as ever, thought Count Bolos. He spoke. "I don't know that I completely trust Corgos. To be honest, I don't know that I trust anyone other than you."

He was not going to mention it, but his master of arms had shown up in one of his nightmares. Those had not diminished, as he and Doctor Heragos had hoped, but had grown even more troubling.

"The captain is a good man," objected Sir Jak. "We might not always see eye to eye, you understand, but I don't question his loyalty."

"Maybe so." He sat a moment, brooding. He should ignore those dreams. As he should ignore Lord Radal's warnings of enemies on all sides.

Lies, all of it. The man was not his friend.

"I may need to use the cottage for other guests," said Bolos, turning their conversation elsewhere. "We'll see how that goes.

"In the meantime, a military company that apparently followed our Sharshite wizard is camped a half-day's march north of us. I gave them my permission but also sent someone to keep an eye on them. My scouts have told me that our former master of arms is camped nearby, also observing."

Hesitantly, knowing his master's dislike for the man, Jak spoke. "Copago is competent."

"I don't like Copago having contact with them. Nor do I want Sir Corgos conferring with him. The two were much too close when both served here.

"Lord Radal has agreed to order them here where we may watch them more closely. I want you to carry the message to their sergeant and see that they set up camp outside our walls." He held out a piece of parchment to the knight.

Is that wise? wondered Jak. He would prefer to have them further away, not nearer.

"Yes, my lord," he answered, taking the paper. "I'll start out right away."

10

The corpulent Gos slouched in his chair, behind a small and untidy desk. "Do not assume that there will be no further attempts at assassination," he warned.

"I do not. It is a constant in the lives of princes."

"Indeed," agreed the chief of Lareth's secret police. "You remain close to Modareth." It was neither a question nor an order, but a statement of fact.

"I do. I will attend one of his salons tomorrow evening. In fact," Pol continued, "his brother and the Princess Mara have for once accepted his invitation."

"I wouldn't expect anything to happen there."

"Perhaps not, sir," agreed the young Arolinian, "but then an enemy might take advantage of such expectations." He smiled wickedly and continued, "I certainly would."

"Not everyone has your imagination, Sir Pol," said Gos. "Thank Jov!"

~ ~ ~

"Lord Radal is my guest. I care not what your king wishes." The count tossed the document he was holding onto the table.

"Certainly, my lord, you are sovereign in your own lands. The king only asks this of you as one ruler to another — one *friend* to another," Doufan assured the count, "and from brotherly concern. The man is dangerous."

Bolos sighed wearily. "This I know, Lord Doufan. It is why he is confined in the tower where I can keep an eye on him."

"It has been shown, sir, that towers may not hold Radal."

"If the sorcerer does somehow flee then I am rid of him and no harm to me." The slightest and most fleeting of smiles appeared on the count's face. Then he spoke more seriously. "But he came here for a reason and I intend to find it out."

The two sat at a table in the Great Hall, empty now save for a sentry at the door. Count Bolos would allow no other, not his wife, not his master of arms. Nor did he show the ambassador any signs of hospitality, permitting him to come here and nowhere else in the keep.

At least he might have offered me a drink, thought Doufan. He's even more parsimonious than his father. Or maybe he just hopes I'll feel unwelcome and leave.

"Nafal has returned from your uncle's," said Lord Doufan.

"And my brother. I am aware what goes on in my county, sir." He shook his head. "I am sorry for my brusqueness, Doufan. This all revolves around Donzalo. This I know. I do not know why."

Should I tell him? wondered the ambassador. He wasn't sure he knew all the story himself.

"What else I know," continued Bolos, "is that Sorsen and Mussago have turned their men around and now lurk on my borders. I know also that your king has been massing troops. I will not turn Radal over to anyone under such circumstances."

He rose from the bench. "I have but one more thing to say, Lord Doufan. If Donzalo is with you, warn him not to come here. There are too many dangers and, I fear, not only for him."

Count Bolos beckoned to the guard. "Escort the ambassador to the stables.

"I will call for you if I wish to speak again," he said to Doufan, and abruptly left the hall, leaving the letter from King Lareth lying where he had dropped it.

~ ~ ~

"Ride with me to Sorsen's camp," spoke Sir Blen. "It is little more than a day distant."

"It does you no good to sit here," added Guesare.

"I should go to the keep. That is why I came home." Donzalo looked toward the ceiling. "And I should be part of what is going on up there. Bolos is my brother."

In his office, a floor above them, Lord Doufan conferred with Jobareth Nafal and the Anian, Oder. Doufan, not surprisingly, had known — or, at least, suspected — who the spy-master was truly and felt it wise to include him.

"A council with Sorsen and Mussago would also be important," responded Blen. "Your uncle and the ladies might be here by the time we return and then we can make further plans."

If nothing else, a journey south would be a way of diverting the young knight from his intention to ride into Castle Rosam, whether welcome or not. All their group had been agreed on this.

"Perhaps," agreed Donzalo. "Not that I trust Sorsen and his father to have the interests of my family at heart."

"Then all the better that you should keep an eye on them, lad," said the minstrel.

The young nobleman shrugged. "Very well. When do we leave?"

~ ~ ~

"I tell you, Captain, the count knows we are encamped here. We only await orders." Dovolo surveyed his camp from this vantage point. He would have thought to put a sentry up here were he not so busy running back and forth from Castle Rosam. It was a mistake to trust in his second to do things right.

"Your company has done plenty enough harm elsewhere for me to hang them all. I know they are the men who attacked my master's manor last year."

The sergeant slowly nodded. "That is true, Sir Copago, but I and many of the others were not with them at that time." He turned to face his companion. "Most of my men are common ruffians, I know. I have tried to bring some discipline to them since taking command."

He glanced toward Copago's well-ordered camp. Not enough discipline to ever take on this bunch, even with an advantage in numbers.

"See to it you have a document with the count's signature on it if you move your men," came Copago's curt reply. "If you do otherwise, we shall attack."

"Understood, Captain."

Sir Copago gazed out across the forested hills. The leaves were now past their peak autumn color and many were falling. He should be back at Paren's manor, attending to all the many tasks of the season. Land needed clearing so they could put in more orchard before spring, peaches and pecans, and there was that hillside that would serve well as a vineyard.

"Hold a minute," he called after Dovolo, who had begun descending the hill. "Riders come."

Three men had entered Copago's camp, soldiers clad in the green and sable of Rosam — the colors he had worn not so long ago. He recognized one as Sir Jak, sergeant of the count's personal guard, and raised a hand in greeting.

"Ho, Sir Copago," called the burly soldier, dismounting. "I've a message for the rabble down there." He nodded his head toward those below them.

"This is their headman, Dovolo." The fellow had returned to stand beside him and held out his hand to take the document Jak held. So he can read, thought Copago, as well as have the bearing of a gentleman. The man may once have been more than a leader of outlaws.

Dovolo perused the parchment and then handed it to Copago. "Here's the document you said I must have, sir. I'll go get my men ready to march."

Copago cursed and looked up at Jak. The soldier's stolid expression revealed nothing. "We will accompany you part way, Sir Jak. I don't like the idea of you three riding with these villains. But I must turn aside before we reach Keep Rosam."

"I will welcome your presence, Sir Copago. Sometimes —" The man hesitated. He had never been a friend of Copago. "Sometimes, I wish that you still served there."

Copago smiled thinly. "As do I, sometimes. And sometimes I am thankful that I do not."

~ ~ ~

"My duty is to follow the count, my lady, whatever I might think of his orders. I can not and will not do otherwise."

"But what, Sir Corgos, if those orders harm my husband? Should we not protect Count Bolos from bad counsel and evil influence?"

151

"That is not mine to question, madame, unless he asks for my opinion."

Lomela dropped wearily onto her divan. "It is good that you are loyal, sir. Know, however, that I fear what lies Lord Radal may be whispering in the count's ear."

The master of arms softened his voice. "My lady, do not believe that I feel differently. I would send the sorcerer back to your father if I could."

"I would send him to hell," came the princess' vehement reply, "where he could harm no one."

She looked up at the knight. "I must trust you to keep an eye on things, Sir Corgos. There is none other in this keep to whom I may turn." Even as she so spoke, she considered how she might bring her husband's faithful Sir Jak to her side or influence this man's wife, the Dame Tiana. But Lomela knew as well that she had planted seeds in his mind that might later yield a crop.

"I will serve as I can, Countess," responded the master of arms, "and attempt to keep you informed."

"I thank you, Sir Corgos. That is all I ask."

~ ~ ~

The old butler was gone. "Lord Doufan sent him off with a pension," said the new caretaker for the embassy's town house. "He felt that a younger man was needed."

The middle-aged fellow was unmistakably a retired soldier, possibly a former sergeant.

"Will it be just the two of you or will young Donzalo be coming as well?" asked he.

"Sir Donzalo is too recognizable to stay around town," replied Guesare. "He remains at the embassy."

The man chuckled. "Recognizable, indeed. I've known him since he was a boy and I served at the keep." He straightened up then, like the military man he was. "You may call me Ubos, good sirs. Sir Guesare and Sir Remare it is?"

"That is correct, Master Ubos," replied Guesare. "Tell me, man, is any of Nafal's good wine about? Remare and I could use a pitcher now, and whatever victuals you might happen to have in your kitchen."

"Certainly, sir," replied the butler and disappeared into his pantry.

"So, what have you been up to, my friend?" asked Guesare.

"Visiting my contacts here, writing dispatches — the usual stuff of a spy's life, Guesare. For once," he said, leaning forward and lowering his voice, "it seems that the empire and Sharsh have a common goal."

"Don't trust Doufan once this is over," warned the Cuddonian. "You know that of course."

"I don't trust him now," replied Oder. He leaned back again as Ubos entered with their wine. "I'll pour," he told him. "You go find us some food, won't you?"

Passing a goblet to Guesare, he continued. "I have become too well known here and, perhaps, everywhere. It is time to give up this life of espionage."

"Will I see you no more?" asked Guesare. He felt a sudden ache in his heart at the thought of losing the man who had been friend, mentor, and lover.

"Who is to say? Perhaps I'll become a diplomat and continue to pull the strings on our web of spies. Or maybe," he said, pausing to sip of his wine, "I shall retire to the family estates. I am a jarl of the empire, you know."

Guesare did not know. He realized he really knew very little of this Anian.

"Perhaps I, too, shall return home," he said, "and stay there this time."

11

"My father has sent you a gift, Sir Donzalo."

"Not another puppy, I hope," replied the young Rosam.

Mussago's lean, leathery face cracked into a genuine smile. "Nay, good sir," he laughed, motioning to a couple of his men to bring forth a small keg. He himself pried the lid off and tipped it so Donzalo might see the contents.

"Gunpowder!"

"That it is. The first to come from your kinsman Daboreth's brimstone. It seems that he and my father have gone into manufacture together." He noted the disappointment on the young man's face. "Be not wrathy toward them, Donzalo. It made good business sense for the counts to collaborate on this. And, moreover," he confided, "Daboreth is soon to be a member of our family. I have given permission for him to wed one of my daughters."

Donzalo shrugged in resignation. "Who am I to disapprove of a man in love?" he asked, and then looked quizzically at Mussago. "How came you to bless such a marriage when you have been far from your home?"

"I have met Daboreth from time to time and know him a good man. When my father approved their match, I readily agreed."

He probably approves anything Mussago the Elder suggests, thought Donzalo. But Dabbi was indeed a good man, and not unlike the one before him. "My congratulations, then," he said with a sincere smile. "We could use a great deal more of that gunpowder."

"We will make you a good price," replied Mussago.

"I must have my men scout County Arvaram for brimstone," mused Sir Sorsen, who had remained silent to that point. "Then we can give you a better price," he stated, but not without a broad wink.

"When all this has settled down, I may be competition for both of you," asserted Donzalo. "Right now, we have other matters to concern us."

"Indeed we do," Blen agreed. "I see the company here has grown."

"Yes," said Mussago. "Another dozen of my father's men came with the powder." He looked to the Sharshite, the man he considered the leader of their group — being quite unwilling to concede such a position to Sorsen, a representative of the rival Arvaram. "Is there nothing we can do but wait here?"

The troops were encamped just below the Rosam border. "I would we were in closer striking distance," added Sorsen. "Even riding hard, it is nearly a day's journey to Ros-town."

"Aye," Mussago said, "and a day more for us to get any news."

"There is a risk," said Sir Blen, "but we could send a man or two north each day to wait in Ros-town. You can provide passports and funds for their lodging, I would assume." He did not add that Sharshite soldiers were already passing from the lands of Count Dordos into County Rosam in just that fashion, and more were on their way across the mountain passes. "It could not be a large force but it would be useful to have men there."

Mussago looked to his fellow captain. "Too bad you are so well known, Sir Sorsen, or you might slip into town yourself."

"Not to mention those fine horses both of you ride," Blen reminded him. "I fear you two will have to remain."

"Well, that's all our business then, isn't it?" asked Donzalo. "What's to eat?"

~ ~ ~

Paren had not hurried. Haste could be left to those who went before him. The reeve's greatest concern had been to get the Lady Fachalana and her companion safely back to Ros-town. Then he would see what could be done for his nephew.

He gave a worried glance at the noblewoman, weary and seemingly dazed, as she rode along. At their somewhat leisurely pace, this journey had stretched to nearly five days. Fachalana soon tired.

"Will we go straight to the castle, sir?" asked Sir Habidros, who had moved up to ride beside him.

"No, I want to get the ladies to the embassy. Lord Doufan can put our small party up for the night." The only others who accompanied them were Master Grippo and a pair of guardsmen.

They passed by the turn toward Keep Rosam. He would take that road soon enough.

~ ~ ~

The soup here was good. Moreover, this little shop was close enough to the embassy's house that he could keep an eye on Guesare and his fellow minstrel, both holed up there. Not too closely, old Doufan had told him — he had a man on the inside for that.

Yes, the minstrel had returned. That was to the good, Perdos told himself, but with things as they were, it would be more difficult than ever to get at him.

He sipped some more of the savory broth from a wooden spoon. Plenty of garlic like they did it back home, and proper dumplings. He felt fortified against the coolness of this day.

There was no point in dawdling here. And they might notice him if he did. Maybe he should seek out Jak again. He'd heard the man had ridden north for the count and returned with Radal's band of ruffians, now camped outside the castle gates. The spot on which his brother had been slain, in fact. He scowled at the thought.

If it were left to him, he would have had a gallows waiting there for them.

Was something going on over there? No, it was only the caretaker off on an errand. Ubos. Perdos remembered him from the castle garrison. Hadn't he been minding the gates on the morning Percos died? He wasn't sure, now.

The knight drained the last from his bowl and set off down the streets of Ros-town.

~ ~ ~

Tiana knew there was no better time to get something from her husband than when both were snug in their bed.

Not because of their love-making — not that it hurt any — but because Corgos so fiercely loved this new settled and wedded life of his. When he held her, she became his whole world, a world that had never been his before, and he forgot the weight of his duties as soldier and captain.

She did not see this as wrong. Tiana was a practical and a realistic woman, and knew that it made sense to use ones advantages.

"Husband," said she, in the darkness, laying her head on his chest. "Our home seems to be in turmoil. Will it be safe for the child?"

She truly did fear for the safety her family, now and future, and believed Corgos would share that concern. And she silently thanked Countess Lomela for speaking to her of these things.

His voice came hesitantly, even reluctantly. "I do not know, my love. The count seems to become ever more unreasonable."

"You could speak to him."

"I should have spoken my thoughts to him before. Now it may be too late." The regret in his voice surprised Dame Tiana.

"Do not blame yourself, husband!"

The master of arms sighed deeply. "In following what I saw as my duty I may have failed my liege. And now I fear to speak lest he come to mistrust me."

I believe he already does, he told himself. This he would not mention to Tiana. She had enough to worry her.

"All I can do," he continued, "is to try to protect Bolos from whatever comes. And if a storm is about to break, my love, it might be best if you were without this castle."

"No, husband," whispered Tiana, "I chose to love a soldier, knowing of his duties. Now I have my duties, too."

~ ~ ~

As such gatherings went, this was a small one. Even for his brother.

But Gawis thanked him for this. Mara should be comfortable with this little group. How long had it been since the two had attended such a salon together? Years, it must be.

There, not surprisingly, was Sir Pol. And the Baroness Ysena, all in gold satin, making eyes at the young knight. He had little doubt that her husband was busy at the buffet.

Once, a youthful Prince Gawis had been the object of Ysena's advances. He had dallied with her for a time, the baron ever unsuspecting. Had Pol cuckolded the old fellow as well?

The prince and his wife passed through the room, murmuring greetings, acknowledging bows, to where stood their host and hostess. The guests seemed to be forming a small crowd at one side of the room, across from the laden tables. My brother provides a good feed, thought Gawis. No wonder his salons are popular.

"Pol is about to read," Carrana informed them.

"From a play?" asked Princess Mara.

"He doesn't know yet, my lady. The boy seems to write these poems with no clear intention for them," said Modareth. "He may attach it to a production later."

Everyone, save a pair of servants at the buffet, turned to listen to Sir Pol.

"This is but a little song," said he, with a smile that was all boyish charm, "for one and all of the ladies present."

I'll hang the moon from a silver chain
to wear beside your heart,
And fashion ear rings of the rain
that drip in subtle art
Against the midnight of your hair
and dawning of your skin —
A glowing, flushing morning fair
with hints of flame within.

Princess Mara thought that he looked directly at her as he spoke, and perhaps he did. Or maybe he was looking at something behind her.

I'll set the sun in a ring of gold
to place upon your hand
And kiss your fingers, making bold
but making no demand;
No, only asking for your love,
that you be mine and stay
Each night of gem-starred sky above,
each jeweled golden day.

As he finished, he spoke loudly over the applause. "Stop that man! He has poisoned the prince's wine!" He pointed toward one of the servitors.

The fellow pulled forth a dagger and sprang toward Prince Modareth. His brother stood in the way. Gawis grappled with the assassin for a moment before the man broke free.

It was enough to keep him from reaching his target. Pol clouted the attacker behind the ear with the pommel of his poniard. He fell to the carpet, dazed.

There was a scream.

On the floor, a pool of red surrounding him, lay the crown prince.

12

Donzalo absently looked about the little common room. He had never been in this cottage when his half-brother and his family had occupied it.

Through the low windows, he could barely see the keep by evening's last light. He might keep an eye on it from here, for now, but he did intend to enter its gates and speak with his brother. Sooner or later, he must.

Bolos had requested that his Uncle Paren stay in this little house rather than Keep Rosam. Too dangerous, he had said, too much going on up there for guests right now.

"It's not so much me he wants to discourage from coming, boy," felt Paren, "as you and your friends. I'm sure he thinks you'll choose to settle in here with me, where he can keep a watch on you at arm's distance."

"And I intend to to keep a watch from closer up," Habidros said. "I may not be your official bodyguard anymore but with that sorcerer scheming up there," he explained, nodding in the direction of the castle, "and his men camped nearby, someone should be looking out for you."

No doubt his brother Guesare — and Oder, too — asked this of him, thought Donzalo. The Cuddonian would surely rather be down in Ros-town with them.

"Are you planning to stay too?" he asked Grippo. "It might get a bit crowded with six of us in here." Paren's two guardsmen were bunking in the cottage as well.

"No, friend Donzalo. I am settled in the embassy as Legate Nafal's secretary and will come here only to bear messages." There was but a tinge of sadness in his voice. "This was my home for many years but that is no longer so. I would rather not be reminded of it."

"Are the ladies well?" Sir Paren asked of him. Fachalana's condition on their ride here had worried him.

"Seemingly, sir. Both are up and about, and the Lady Fachalana is eating enough for two. Practicing her swordsmanship, as well, on anyone foolish enough to fence with her."

Donzalo laughed. "Sir Blen, I think, will always be such a fool."

~ ~ ~

My dream, thought Mara. This was my dream.

Sentries had taken hold of the would-be assassin and Pol was now on his knees beside the prince. "He lives," he reported, holding a finger to his neck to feel the pulse. "Where — where is his wound?" the knight wondered, his hands seeking the source of the blood.

"Oooow," came Gawis's voice, low. "My head hurts!" He opened his eyes. "Modi! Is he safe?"

"I am, my brother, thanks to your defense," said Prince Modareth, who knelt on his other side. "Where are you hurt?"

Gawis held up his left arm. "He gashed my arm. And then I slipped in this damned wine and banged my head on the floor!"

Modareth sniffed at the red pool and then laughed aloud. "My brother bleeds a fine vintage!" He tore open the prince's sleeve. "It does not look too bad. Has anyone sent for a physician?"

"I have, husband," replied the Princess Carrana. "Give them some room!" she ordered their guests who had gathered round, dumbfounded by this turn in the evening's entertainments.

"We must make sure that the dagger was not poisoned," spoke Pol. He doubted it but there was always that chance.

Prince Gawis rose unsteadily to his feet, feeling gingerly at the back of his head. "I may bleed there, too," he said. "I shall most certainly have a great bump."

Princess Mara stood staring at her husband for a moment, before stepping forward to tearfully embrace him. "I feared you dead, my prince," she hoarsely whispered. "I feared you dead but you came back to me!"

He wrapped his uninjured arm about her. "What, would I leave before our child was born? I will not be cheated of that!" He tipped his head down to kiss her brow. That hurts! he thought, and let wife and brother lead him to a chair and the waiting doctor.

~ ~ ~

"Sir Paren wants me to stay here," Copago said. "He had left a message for me with Lady Thara." The master of arms clearly disapproved of his orders. "I should be the one riding to Castle Rosam, not he!"

"What could you do there?" asked the Dame Sima. "You know you are not welcome."

"In a crisis, fighting men are always welcome," he told his mother. "The count may need such."

"Then he should not have sent you away," asserted his wife, Janona, walking on his other side.

"The reeve will send word if he needs you," said Sima. "Paren is certainly capable of making his own decisions." She looked out across a newly-cleared field. "I'll miss the woods that were here."

"The cows won't. We needed more pasture."

"Your son is such a romantic," asserted Janona.

"Don't I know it," replied Sima. "As was his father." For a moment, memories of the late Count Borrago filled the minds of all three.

"I would do right by the legacy of my father," said Copago, at last. "Even if it means defending a brother who hates me."

"And one who loves you, I think," Janona said. "It is Donzalo who stands central to all of this."

"Aye," Sir Copago growled, "I will not abandon that overgrown boy."

~ ~ ~

"This seems far too familiar," said Sir Blen.

"Including the part where Fachalana ever bests you?" teased Ansa.

"That is to be expected, my lady." He looked the slender Anian up and down. "Have you ever fenced? Perhaps I should try crossing swords with you for a change!"

Fachalana laughed at the thought. "Our friend is no

swordswoman. However, I would not wish to come across her in a darkened alley with a dagger in her hand."

Blen soberly nodded his agreement. He had seen what Ansa could do.

"Again, my, er, Fachalana?"

"No, Blen, I have tired." The tall noblewoman returned her blade to its scabbard. "It is my father. He is so near — I ever feel his presence. It wears on me."

"Does he try to speak to you?"

She shook her head. "He knows it would do no good."

He is always with her, inside, thought Blen. Being near the sorcerer must make it all the worse. Would she be freed of him were her father dead or would he live on in her soul?

"There is a place," she went on, speaking as if in a dream, "that I have seen. A place where I might escape all this. When we are done here," Fachalana said, her voice now more resolute, "perchance I might find it again."

Both Blen and Ansa sent silent prayers to their respective deities that such would be.

~ ~ ~

At times now, Bolos would go the tower alone and sit with Lord Radal, trying to solve the riddle of the man.

But it brought only more riddles. Despite the Sharshite's words, he knew he was no friend. What did he want?

And the dreams continued. Now, his brother was showing up in them more frequently and his presence was not a welcome one. Donzalo would never be the bloody usurper he saw in his nightmares.

And surely he shouldn't believe those visions of Lomela's infidelity with his brother.

No, it was simply all else that was weighing on him that caused these fantasies of the night. Radal was right to point out that Bolos's enemies were gathering.

"Who are my enemies?" he asked the man. "Can I trust anyone?"

"A wise ruler trusts none," replied the former lord councilor. "Do not trust me but weigh my words carefully for their truth."

Bolos thought silently on this a while before deciding there was no more to said on the subject. "Are you well, my lord?" he asked Radal. The man seemed frail, though no more now than when he had shown up at the gates of Keep Rosam. Reports were that he ate little and slept almost never.

"No, my Lord Bolos. I am dying." He smiled thinly at the count's reaction. "Not yet; there are things I must do before I leave this world."

~ ~ ~

"Where is Donzalo this morning?"

"He was here but a minute ago," replied one of the soldiers, "finishing up his breakfast."

"And quite a breakfast it was," said the other. "I think he stepped outside."

Habidros cursed himself for sleeping in. And he cursed the young Laman as a fool for taking a walk without his protection. Didn't he know Lord Radal's cutthroats were just down the road?

No breakfast for him. He hurried out the door to catch up with his charge.

Around the cottage he went to the small stable, overcrowded with the mounts of his companions. There, Donzalo was saddling his own.

"Where to, lad?" asked the Cuddonian.

"Home," came the reply. "It is time to speak with my brother."

It was bound to come to this, sooner or later, Habidros told himself. "I'll ride with you."

"Thank you, Habi. I doubt you will be permitted to enter."

"Then we shall part at the gate. Are you sure of this?"

"No," said Donzalo, leading his horse into the open yard. "But that makes no difference. Let's ride."

13

"Our foremost concern," said Lord Doufan, "is to protect the Lady Lomela and her son. Beyond that, the goals are flexible."

Jobareth Nafal was discouraged. "Can we truly have any effect on things here, my lord?" he asked the ambassador.

Doufan, to the surprise of neither Jobareth nor Blen, had a ready answer. "History is a runaway horse and most of the time all we can do is to hold on. But now and then, perhaps, we may find ourselves able to give a little tug on the reins and turn it, ever so slightly, in our desired direction."

"I think, sir, we are more likely to fall off and be trampled," said Sir Blen, half-jestingly. Such a quip from the reserved knight *was* a bit of a surprise.

"Indeed, my good sir," agreed the elder diplomat, "yet we must try to ride. That is why we three are met here in what amounts to a council of war. This is why we must discuss plans to defeat Radal."

He leaned against the front of his oversize desk, facing the two men as though he were a schoolmaster and asked a seemingly unrelated question of Jobareth. "Tell me, Nafal, what is the purpose of government?"

"Sir, my father would say it is to maintain and protect the roads."

Doufan chuckled. "That, indeed, sounds like him. But such are means, not ends."

"To see that everyone is treated fairly," suggested Blen, sounding at once earnest and uncertain.

His companions looked at each other with a certain incredulity and then began to laugh.

"The purpose of government is to help create and maintain a stable society," stated Lord Doufan. "All else serves that end.

"Now admittedly, Sir Blen, a fair government can, more often than not, best fulfill that task. But it can not let itself be a slave to such ideals."

"Nor to ideologies of any sort," said Jobareth. "I know that school of thought. I am not sure though, my lord, if I agree with it."

"It is not a popular philosophy at the universities," admitted the ambassador.

Blen, after a moment's thought, said, "It makes sense to me."

"You are a practical man. Nafal here is a poet and dreamer. As," he continued, "is our Lord Radal. Yes, Radal," he maintained, noting the doubtful expressions of his companions. "The man is the worst sort of romantic. He believes in power and all it can accomplish.

"The lord councilor has always been committed to the centralized power of his king. It goes beyond a personal loyalty to Lareth. It is his philosophy, even his creed, one might say."

"Power does have its uses," opined Jobareth.

"Yes, lad, it does. But too much power with one man or group is dangerous. I have always believed there should be a balance."

"Balance seems to be *your* philosophy of life, my lord," Blen quietly commented.

Doufan nodded in acknowledgment to his statement. "Balance and stability is what we must seek here in Lama, whatever our means might be."

He again addressed Nafal. "Legate," he said. Neither man recalled him ever using his subordinate's title previously. "I must ask you about your relationship to Lord Radal. He was your patron and his daughter is your supposed fiancée. Will this have any bearing on where your loyalties lie?"

"Our intended engagement was always a ruse, sir. There is no promise between Lady Fachalana and myself other than one of friendship."

Blen, although he gave no sign, was most interested to learn this.

"Moreover," continued Jobareth, "I long since pledged my loyalty to Princess Lomela over that of Radal."

"Very well. We need a way to contact the princess, and all those who dwell within the castle walls, since we have been shut out. Communication is key to any successful campaign."

166

"I know of one who might help us pass messages, sir," said Blen. "Sir Copago once told me of a certain laundress who visits regularly."

"She is readily bribed?"

"Better yet, my lord, she has a personal loyalty to the count and could easily be persuaded that we are trying to help him."

Should I tell what I know, what was entrusted to me by Donzalo? wondered Jobareth Nafal. How better to help him?

He spoke. "And I know of a secret way into the keep."

~ ~ ~

There would be no more from Jak. Count Bolos had shut the gates of his keep and none entered nor left, except on his direct order.

"You're a northerner, aren't you?" asked the woman who filled his bowl. Perdos nodded. From her accent, he recognized that she was as well.

"I have something here you might like," said she, setting a chipped earthenware plate before him.

He recognized the soft, garlicky cheese immediately, as much by its odor as its appearance. "Oulg! I haven't had any since I was a boy." Such memories it brought to him.

The woman laughed at his broad grin. "A northern boy, indeed!" she said, cutting him a generous slice. "I was afraid I would have to eat all of this myself as none here appreciate it. I am Rassana."

"You have none with whom to share it, Dame Rassana?"

"Mistress Rassana. My man left me and I have kept this shop as best I can on my own."

He leaned in close to her. "My name is Perdos but I ask you not to speak it loudly. There are those about who, um, do not wish me well."

"Very well, Master Perdos," she whispered in reply.

"Sir Perdos, actually." Why did he feel it necessary to impress her with his knighthood?.

She smiled. It was a very nice smile, he thought. "I shall call you Dorbi," she said. "That was my dog's name back in Flosa."

167

"Flosa? Why, I grew up only a few leagues from there. Over on the river."

Rassana cut two more slices of oulg, one for each. "You are watching that house over there."

Perdos nodded.

"Considering all the goings on in that place, I'm surprised more don't watch it."

"Maybe they do," laughed Perdos. "Maybe they're just better at it than I am."

"Well, Dorbi, feel free to watch from my counter anytime." She smiled again at him. "Anytime at all."

~ ~ ~

He could not leave now, not with how things stood in Lama. But these were serious events in the capital. His heir wounded while protecting his younger brother! That was not something Lareth might ever have dreamed of occurring.

Gawis should be here with him. It was never good to have two sons in the same town, much less the same room, and possibly lose both at once. Yes, he would send for the crown prince. Maybe he could learn something of ruling during this crisis.

And maybe his son could handle such a crisis himself the next time and let his old father take things easy in Celatas. The chill of Mountain Keep did not agree with him.

It would not do to be here in the dead of winter. Although the pass was rarely closed, it had been known to occur and then he would be cut off from his kingdom across the mountains.

Whatever was going to happen in Lama, it must happen soon.

~ ~ ~

"I like the countess well enough," said Aulla. "She knows my past and does not hold it against me. A true gentlewoman she is, not like some of those who grew up in these parts." The laundress looked at the cloak she held. "This is a fine puke, sir. Cuddonian?"

"The fabric is, Dame Aulla. The garment was cut in Celatas."

"Ah. 'Twill take special care." She looked up from the cloth. "So you wish to know of me and the count, do you?"

Lord Doufan nodded. "Only what you wish to tell me, madame, but the more I know, the better may I help the man."

She seemed satisfied with that answer. "Bolos danced the jig with me as a youth and left me with child." She nodded in the direction of a little girl, playing quietly with her doll amid the heaps of laundry. "He has since done well by us. Of course, I have a husband now and he is not too bad a sort. Lazy, but so it goes."

"Your own industry seems to make up for it."

Aulla laughed. "Aye, sir, and all the business of the castle being sent my way. I don't even have to get my own hands wet anymore!"

"And you, then, come and go in the keep as you will?"

"No one questions me, but I do have a regular schedule. I always attend to things personally up there."

The woman was short, broad of build and face. She seems quite ordinary, thought Doufan. He suspected that Aulla affected such a persona, even as did he.

"Then you will be able to pass messages to and from Countess Lomela and others." The ambassador made certain his voice expressed approval and, even, admiration. Subtle flattery was never a bad idea. "The count needs friends and I am sure we can consider you one of them. But know," he continued, "that we will not fail to reward you in other ways."

Aulla, after all, did not become a successful businesswoman purely on sentiment.

~ ~ ~

"Do you remember Mother?" asked Bolos, of a sudden. It seemed an odd subject to bring up just then.

"I do, though I fear I would not know her face now."

"You were what, six, at the time she died? I remember how much you cried because you were not permitted to see her."

"It was the plague, wasn't it? No wonder Father didn't want me there."

169

"Nay, it was the grippe. It was widespread that year. Many died, some of them my friends." He paused for a moment, holding and then releasing old memories. "I was stricken too, but lived. If things had been but a bit different, you might be count now."

No, our father would would still be count, Donzalo said to himself. To Bolos he said, "Histories say that plagues broke the Ani ambitions in the west as much as any force of arms."

"You and your books." Bolos shook his head. "Are they all intact up at Uncle Paren's place?"

"They are." He let his gaze sweep the mostly empty suite he occupied, the one he had vacated a few months earlier. "I might as well have left them here. They would help me pass the time."

Bolos recognized the mild accusation. "I only hope to keep you safe here until we can get all this sorted out. You — you did right to give me that clout. I hold it not against you."

"But it was not necessary, Brother. I let anger move me."

"You acted like the fighting man you have become. You are no longer the boy you were not long ago."

I am very far from that boy, now, thought Donzalo.

"Lord Radal tells me I should distrust you, Donzalo," said the count. "I do not believe this. I can not believe this. But why is he your enemy?"

"Radal blames me for the death of one who was important to him." He stared at the floor for a moment, before raising his eyes to his brother. "But she was more important to me. I loved her, Bolos, and lost her to darkness."

"In the Cuddon?" He had heard rumors.

Donzalo only nodded his head slowly. Bolos saw his hand go the curious brooch he had ever worn this past year. It is best I ask no more, he told himself.

The younger man sighed and straightened himself up. "But know also that the sorcerer and his king saw me as a threat to you. That is what started all this."

STEPHEN BROOKE

So it goes back to Donzalo being a danger again, thought the count. There seemed no getting away from that.

And there seemed to be no true answers

"I won't keep you confined to this room," said Bolos, "though Lord Radal thinks you should be in the tower rather than he. Go where you will in the keep, as long as the guards accompany you." Keeping in mind Donzalo's mysterious disappearance from his previous captivity — another puzzle — the count had made certain that this brother was ever within sight of two guardsmen, even in his own rooms. "Visit Lomela. She would enjoy seeing you."

Then he frowned at a sudden thought. "Everywhere but the tower, Donzalo. I do not think you should be in the same room as Radal."

~ ~ ~

"We have had our differences, Sir Jak."

"Forget it, Corgos," said Jak. "None of it was all that important."

"No, it wasn't," agreed the master of arms. "Not compared to what is happening now."

He poured out more red wine for the both of them. Cheap stuff, thought Jak. Probably the sort of drink Sir Corgos became used to during his days as a mercenary. Himself, he'd rather have a beer.

"What can we do?" he asked. "Or maybe the question is what *should* we do?"

"I wish I knew. I don't want to go against the count."

"We may have to." Jak leaned forward and spoke earnestly. "Count Bolos is not only my liege — he is my friend. I have a duty there too."

"Yes, Jak, I know of your friendship," Corgos replied with the trace of a smile. "I suppose that was the cause of some of the friction between us. How long have you been with the man?"

"Since he's been a man," responded the burly knight, taking a gulp of his wine. "Count Borrago made me his bodyguard better'n ten years ago." Jak put a hand to the top of his bald head. "I even had hair back then. Some, anyway," he laughed.

171

"You know the count better than anyone, eh? Then you're best suited to keeping an eye on him."

Jak nodded. "And you're the fellow for organization. I know I'm not good at running things."

"I suspect that our wives and the countess may actually be running things," said Sir Corgos, raising his glass. "And I salute them."

14

Indeed, I should not be in the same room with Radal, thought Donzalo, for only one of us would leave it alive. He would not hesitate to put a blade into the man, given the opportunity.

The Donzalo of only a year ago would not have considered such a thing.

"Must you come in with me?" he asked his two guards.

"Those are the orders," one replied. The other nodded in agreement.

"Well, at least stay on the other side of the room so we can have a private conversation."

The two looked at each other. Clearly their orders were not specific about how close they should remain to their charge. "Very well, sir," said one. "But if you go into another room, we'll follow."

What would happen if I went out on Lomela's balcony? he wondered.

Dame Traspa opened the door to him and his companions. The pair of soldiers took up a station just inside.

"How is married life, my dear?" asked Donzalo, as he embraced the maid.

"Tolerably good, young sir," she responded, "though I miss the attention I used to get from the kitchen staff."

"You should flirt a little with them and make Sir Jak jealous," he told her. Lomela was rising from a seat beneath the window to greet him and, beside her, the master of arms' wife. Donzalo realized that he barely knew the woman.

"My lady." He took Lomela's hand but did not embrace her. He remembered the consequences when last he held the princess in his arms. "Dame Tiana." He gave her a small bow.

"Come sit with us, Donzalo," said the Lady Lomela. "You, too, Traspa. You are our best informant."

"Yes," agreed Tiana, turning to the maid. "Tell him what you were just saying to us about Radal."

"My Jak has heard that man whispering to the count that Corgos is untrustworthy and was the one who released you," said Traspa, as she settled on a low stool by their divan.

Tiana gave him a quizzical look. "We still wonder how you managed that, sir."

"I am afraid you must continue to do so, Dame Tiana. Secrets cease to be secrets when too many know them."

Donzalo has learned to talk like a statesman, thought Lomela. Perhaps to think like one, as well.

"We have a note for you," she said, handing him a folded paper. "There is a way to get messages in and out."

He opened it and quickly read. "In Nafal's hand but no doubt written by committee," he said with a smile. "Nothing of actual importance in it." He casually handed it back. "Best burn it after I leave. If I did so now it might make my two friends watching at the door suspicious."

"They report to my husband," Tiana said, "and he's in on this."

Donzalo nodded. "If only I could make my brother see the dangers of harboring that sorcerer, we would need not plot."

"I fear you are not the one who has his ear," responded Lomela, "nor am I."

"There are bad times coming, my lady," opined the Dame Traspa, shivering involuntarily at the thought. "I'm sure of it."

Tiana took her hand. "We can only do our best to be ready for them, my friend."

And hope we can survive the crisis, Lomela thought. She feared that not all those she loved would.

"Enough of conspiracy," she said, as gaily as she could. "Donni, you must tell me all about your time at Sir Paren's keep. And how fared the Lady Fachalana?"

~ ~ ~

Dorbi seemed a good name. Short for Dorbidros, maybe? Well, probably not short for anything if it was given to a dog.

Anyway, I'll use it, decided Perdos. It's better than 'Dos.'

He surveyed the camp before him. Not much going on there. Maybe the count had done well to have these men where he could keep watch on them.

Beyond them, down the road, lay the cottage where Sir Paren's group stayed. The knight wondered if he could ride by these men without anyone recognizing him. Not that he had any reason to. Paren and that brother of Guesare — what was his name? — could take care of themselves. Nor would they welcome Perdos to their lodging.

Maybe if he hung around here long enough, the minstrel would ride up here to visit. But it seemed unlikely; more likely they would make council down at the Sharshite embassy. There was too much going on around here, anyway, to seek a duel with the Cuddonian right now.

Best he wait until this current crisis ended, one way or another, and continue to serve the ambassador. If that man opposed Radal and his followers, then Perdos felt he had chosen the correct side.

And he would not mind at all hanging about Mistress Rassana's shop while attending to his duty.

~ ~ ~

The boy was so close, yet still beyond his reach.

Using magic against him was out of the question, at least for now. He could not be certain of its success and any great magic now would surely end his life. There was too little left of Lord Radal.

Better that Bolos be responsible for the deed or, failing that, one of his own men. He needed to get them inside the castle walls, one way or another.

To that end, he might manage some minor magics. Gates could be opened, guardsmen could sleep. Radal had noted the seals placed on the portals when he had entered the keep — the work of Guesare, he assumed. They were well enough done but would not withstand his mastery.

First, he must have Dovolo smuggle his ebony cask in to him. With the object of power it held at hand, he could better prepare for such work. He needed a staff, as well. Any stick would do. There was no potency to the rod itself; it only acted as means to further focus his strength.

Radal smiled. Surely Count Bolos would provide an old man a staff on which he might lean. He must speak to him of it the next time they met. Yes, of that and of many things, for imposing his will on the mind of Bolos was his true work here.

It was work that was going well.

~ ~ ~

"Thank you, Doo." Pol turned toward his manservant so that the fellow could read his lips. He then dismissed him with a few signs that he had learned. Who would have known that the deaf had their own language?

The young Arolinian had immediately recognized the usefulness of sign language to one who engaged in espionage. When he became more skilled, he intended to instruct a few chosen men in it.

He set the cup Doo had brought him on his desk and went to poke at the fire. Nights were becoming more than cool now, though he was told that winter was never that bad in Celatas. Certainly nothing like his native province in the north.

His thoughts turned to the Princess Mara and her reactions to the occurrences of a few evenings ago. It was as if it had all seemed familiar to her in some fashion, as if she were reliving the events.

As if she were an actor in one of his plays, he thought, and smiled at the idea.

The voice of Murbalana was raised outside the door, scolding someone. Murbalana provided excellent material for his writing. Pol did hope that she remained with the imperturbable Doo. Maybe even marry the man.

Mara. He should cultivate her. Oh, the prince too, of course. Wouldn't his parents, the simple shopkeepers, have been astounded by the heady company their son now kept?

For a moment, his heart became a lump in his chest as he remembered them, dead now half a decade. Then, an idea for the play on which he was working popped into his mind.

Pol went to his desk, took up his pen and began writing.

~ ~ ~

Fachalana practiced her magic. Yes, it tired her but how else was she to learn? If only she had books!

It was the link that she worked on, mostly. That she knew how to do, more or less, but she needed more experience, needed to make all of it as natural to her as wielding a sword. Her mind poked into many worlds, but not too deeply. Lady Fachalana had quickly learned caution.

Fortunately, it was not needed to enter those dangerous places to form the link. There were little empty worlds suited for such purposes, where two sorcerers might meet and speak. She had so spoken to several now, some of them lost, mad souls who did not understand their gift and had wandered into other worlds unintentionally. Without her father's hand to guide her, might she have been so?

Had that been the fate of her grandmother?

There had been those who, as had once her father, tried to take control of her. She was too strong for that now, too knowledgeable. Indeed, she could have overwhelmed any of them had she so chosen.

Daughter of Radal, came a voice, seemingly very far away.

It was like the voices she had heard when she fought against her father's power, the voices that said they could no longer protect her.

Are you the Fay? she asked.

I am of the Fay, came the answer, stronger now that she opened herself to this link. *I am Arsel*. The voice hesitated. *You are so much like your sister. But you are different, as well.*

He knew Jola, she thought. Could he hear her say that in her mind? If so, the fay did not reveal it.

Your are ones who gave me shelter, said Fachalana. *I can no longer find that place.*

It is closed to thee now. When your trials are done, you may come to us and, perhaps, find it again.

Trials?

You must face the struggle that is to come, your battle against the Darkness. We will try but I fear we can not help thee in this. The fay was silent for long moments. Had he left her? *Donzalo holds that which may strengthen thee. Verily, it may be your salvation.*

What is that? she asked.

You will know it when the time comes. The voice of Arsel seemed filled with concern. *You are wearied. Rest and prepare yourself.*

And he was gone.

~ ~ ~

"Sir Paren says there have been reports of riders on our borders."

"Sorsen and his bunch? We know about them," said the count, putting down his spoon.

"No, my lord, this was a report from his master of arms." Corgos felt it best not to refer to the man by name. "Troops moving in the Cuddon."

"Cuddonians?" Bolos found the idea doubtful. Once, of course, bandits had raided from those hills but there had been peace for decades.

"Or Ani. Or both. Remember the thanes of the Cuddon recognize the Anian emperor as their overlord."

More enemies. They seek to surround me, Bolos told himself. "Surely the Ani would not invade Lama." He did not feel so sure.

"More likely, my husband, they are worried about the situation here," spoke the Countess Lomela. "If Sharsh or An Corade were to get involved, the empire might react."

Sir Corgos nodded in agreement. Lady Lomela grasped these matters better than any other in the keep.

"Indeed," she continued, "they might prove to be allies."

"What, against your father?"

"My loyalty now lies with County Rosam, Bolos. We have a son," Lomela reminded him. "I would think it unlikely that Ani troops would come into Lama. That would not keep them from using Cuddonian surrogates."

"Your brother has friends in the Cuddon," pointed out Sir Corgos.

"Hmm, yes." Bolos was uncertain whether that was a good thing or a bad one. "My own men report more Sharshite soldiers slipping over the mountains and finding their way to our borders. And Count Dordos is surely poised to take advantage of any turmoil. There are disputed lands he would wish to claim." Or even those not disputed.

"Altogether too many strange men loiter about the town as well, my lord," reported Corgos.

"I must depend on my captain there," said the count. On whom should he depend here? Corgos? Jak?

He turned to the lunch he was sharing with these two, here in the tower room that was once his father's office, now that of Sir Corgos. One floor above him, there was another. Was Lord Radal someone in whom he might ever trust? He must speak with him again later.

And he would take the man the new walking stick he had promised him.

15

Mussago was completely willing to sit and wait. This did not agree with Sorsen's temperament; he became impatient.

"If I take a different horse, I could slip into Ros-town," he told his fellow commander.

"You're still recognizable," said Mussago. "Not just your looks but your manner."

Sorsen sighed. He knew it was true. The nobleman poured himself more hot cider. The wind was cold today.

"What has your father to say?" asked his companion. A message had arrived minutes earlier. "I hope he is not sending more troops, for then my father would feel it necessary to do the same. I'd rather they were getting the harvest in."

"None now, Master Mussago," answered Sorsen, "but he has them on alert. He says the Coradeans are mobilizing too, moving more men to the mainland and to Sharsh's southern border."

"They would rather use your Arvaram troops here than send their own into Lama."

"Aye. I would not expect an invasion. But I should think my father will be concerned now about having Coradeans on his own border and be less likely to send any more men north."

Mussago nodded. "As my own worries about all the Sharshite men across the Doram Pass."

"I think perhaps," replied Sorsen, "that your father the count would not greatly mind his lands being a part of Sharsh."

"It might well be good for business," agreed Mussago.

~ ~ ~

Lord Radal opened his iron-bound cask. Within lay the skull of his long-dead master, a mighty object of power.

With this and the small grimoire he carried always upon his person, he could prepare great magics. Oh, and the staff, of course. The sorcerer would have preferred the familiar, heavy ebon rod he had of necessity left behind in Mountain Keep, but this stick provided by Count Bolos would do. Hickory, wasn't it?

Dovolo had done well, concealing the vessel between his legs and slipping it out even while a soldier stood guard in his chamber. Who would have thought to look up the man's kilt, especially in that he had come to the tower before without incident? Too bad he couldn't bring in a sword that way. Radal might need seek one in some other world.

Soon. The new moon might lend assistance to his strength — darkness was an ally both on the physical and mystic planes. There was much to plan before then, seals to set, seals to break.

"Give me strength for this final task, Lord Asak," he whispered, "and then you may take me."

~ ~ ~

A group of men crowded around Sir Blen, Lord Doufan among them.

"If the cuts are of proper depth," he explained, "the bombe will fly apart evenly when it explodes, throwing shards of metal in all directions." The knight held up the grenade he had been preparing.

"This is a talent I did not know you possessed," remarked the ambassador. "I might have expected it of Sir Copago or even our friend Donzalo."

Blen looked up at the man and smiled. "In truth, sir, I saw the design in papers young Donzalo had in his quarters."

"Oh, there is our laundress. I must speak to her of my tunics." Aulla's cart had drawn up to the wide, arched ground-floor entry to the embassy. "You wished to have words with Dame Aulla too, didn't you Sir Blen?"

"Yes, my lord. Carry on here, men."

"Do you think these bombes will prove useful?" asked Doufan, as the two walked to where the laundress and her hired man unloaded bundles of clean, folded garments. Most of the cart was taken up by the unwashed laundry of Keep Rosam, their previous stop.

"Who is to say, sir? Any weapon is only as good as the man who wields it."

"I could not have stated it any better, Sir Blen. Hail to you, Dame Aulla."

"Good morn to you, my lord. I'll have all your wash loaded up and be away in a nonce." She leaned close to the ambassador and whispered, "Your messages are in with your tunics, my lord."

He nodded and replied in a low voice, "I've none to pass the other way on this day." More loudly he said, "You must come up to my office on the morrow and we shall speak of our account."

"Understood, sir," she countered, with the ghost of a wink, and turned to her loading of dirty linens.

~ ~ ~

Jobareth felt as if he were a child listening to grownups when Oder and Lord Doufan conversed.

He suspected that his friends felt the same. The young diplomat glanced at Habidros and Guesare. They barely seemed to be paying attention.

Ubos silently refilled their cups.

Nafal had ridden down to Ros-town with the ambassador only an hour earlier, Habidros accompanying them as their only bodyguard. Doufan would have no others, thinking it would bring too much notice.

Now they spoke of things beyond Jobareth's knowledge, of diplomats and generals and goings-on in distant courts.

Of a sudden, Oder posed a quite unexpected question to Lord Doufan. "Have you been dallying with Dame Aulla?" The brothers certainly showed interest at that. Jobareth was rather taken aback by the suggestion.

The Sharshite shrugged and smiled amiably. "I have taken my pleasure there, yes. And, yes, before you scold me, I know the dangers in so mixing my secrets.

"Perhaps you should know also — especially you, Sir Guesare — that I have secret dealings with another."

"Perdos?" asked Oder. "We have seen him watching from the little food stall down the street. Though lately his eyes have been more on his hostess there than on us."

"I felt it wise to tie him to our cause rather than have him wandering masterless. Who knows what mischief he might have gotten into, left to his own devices?"

Guesare nodded, but seemed none too convinced.

There was a clatter in the street — most unusual in this neighborhood, at this hour. Someone had been riding hard and now hurried up the stairs. The steward went to the door to admit Sir Blen.

The knight paused a moment to catch his breath, and reported. "Radal's men are in the keep!"

~ ~ ~

It had been swift and bloodless. Mostly. One fool from the garrison had managed to be in the wrong place and had his throat slit as a result.

Now, he and his troop had a tenuous control of the keep. Or, at least, they had the count and none would dare act against them. If only this Corgos would give the boy up to them or Count Bolos would order it, they could be done with this business.

Dovolo had most of his men here at the tower, save for a few guarding the gates. It didn't hurt to have someone on watch, even if their chief concern was with those already within the keep. If any approached, they could send up an alarm.

Someone was opening the door to the Great Hall. Hadn't they all been told to stay within? Oh, it was that dolt, Jak. Lord Radal had made him their messenger boy.

It was fortunate that he had been the only one with the count when he and the men had taken the tower. Or maybe it was not fortune at all, but his master's planning. Had they not been sitting with the wizard, ready for the taking?

Well, that was beyond him. All he knew was that gates had been unbarred, men had slept or been locked in their quarters, and it had been easy entry for him and the boys.

And that this place was ripe for plundering. Maybe when Lord Radal finished with his own affairs he would turn them loose.

~ ~ ~

"Wake, Sorsen!"

The knight rolled over. Mussago? He was instantly alert. "The time has come?"

"It has. Radal has seized Keep Rosam and holds Bolos hostage."

Sorsen had slept in his tunic since encamping here, so he might be on horseback all the more quickly. "Leave the tents and luggage," he ordered, as he emerged from his pavilion. "We ride at once!"

In minutes, they were racing north. Mussago handed the message to his companion, that he might read it in the saddle. Behind them, the courier sped southward on a fresh horse with his news, to alert both their sires.

Sorsen gave it a quick look. "We are the closest. Even so, our friends may choose to act before we can arrive." It was late morning now; they could not hope to reach Ros-town before dawn.

"It is good that we sent some men ahead of us," stated Mussago.

"There are Sharshite soldiers across the Weldar, too. Sir Blen may call them to him."

"And in a few days, Lareth himself will be informed. Who knows how he might act?"

"All the more reason for us to handle it ourselves, and quickly." They rode on for a time, the only sound that of their horses' hooves.

Then spoke Sorsen again. "It will take too long, I fear, for Copago to respond. He would have been a good man to have beside us."

"Aye," agreed Mussago, "if we be not too late ourselves."

16

Radal had found a deck of cards in the room and had used it to fill his hours while held captive. It lay now on the table, no longer of any use to him.

Bolos noted it. "Is it so that one can read the future in the cards? Tell me of mine."

Radal regarded the man across the table for a moment, before taking up the deck. "Am I to be your fortune-teller, my lord?" The idea briefly brought a smile to his gaunt face. "The cards can not see the future, nor can I. What they do is provide us symbols, structure for our thoughts." He shuffled and laid out three cards between them, one above the other two.

"This is sometimes known as the ziggurat," said the sorcerer. "The two cards at the bottom speak of the forces in action and those in opposition. That atop them is a possible resolution." He looked up from the spread. "Only possible."

"Ziggurat? What means the word?"

"Some so name their temple mounds. The Kamatians of the south where they speak the Baxac languages." Radal returned to the cards. "We may not see the future but those with the proper gifts might glimpse into the timeless void where all things be. So works prophecy."

His long fingers touched the first card in the bottom row. "The Knight of Chalices. That might be your brother. And this," he said, pointing to that beside it, "the Ten of Blades." Radal considered the card for a brief while. "A card of disruption, perhaps, of plans gone awry."

No, he told himself, the Knight may not be Donzalo at all, but my long-time opponent, Guesare. I am this other, the old man, the troubled mind.

"Here at the top, the Ace of Torches." All too obviously my daughter, he thought, full of fire and promise. A promise of her survival? "A sign of success and new beginnings," he half-lied.

"Yours or mine?" asked the count, with enough sarcasm to surprise the sorcerer. He didn't know Bolos had it in him.

But he had already proven more difficult to manipulate than Lord Radal had expected.

There came a knock at the door. "Enter," called the Sharshite. Count Bolos turned in his chair to see who it was and then rose to embrace his sergeant and friend Maybe, thought Radal, I can turn the servant if the master remains difficult.

"Ah, the faithful Sir Jak," he said, with all the easy grace of a courtier. "Do sit and join us in our lunch."

~ ~ ~

"We must continue to work in secret," asserted Oder. "The Rosam captain here in town would not permit us to act nor would he will-ingly accept orders from a Sharshite. Nor," he continued, with a wry smile, "an Anian."

Sir Blen agreed, though he harbored many doubts about this spy who had joined their group. "He will do nothing for fear of harm coming to the count. And he is on alert for any activity. My lord" said he to Lord Doufan, "I have passed the word for our men to assemble here at the embassy."

"Tonight?" asked the ambassador.

"Tonight would be best. Donzalo's life is in danger every minute we wait, as are those of all in Castle Rosam." He turned to Jobareth Nafal. "We depend on you, sir. Only you know this secret way in."

Jobareth glanced at Oder. Did the mysterious Anian know of it? "Sir Copago holds this knowledge as well," he informed them. "If I meet mishap, turn to him."

"I fear he may arrive too late for it to matter," spoke Sir Paren. "It is a long way to my manor and a long ride back. Moreover, he may need tend to affairs there, if some of the rumors have it aright."

"Your master of arms need fear no threat from the east," Oder assured him. "Of this I am certain."

Having been told all his life to never trust the Ani, Paren was not at all assured.

"There can be no more messages to nor from the keep, so we may only guess at how things stand there. But," said Lord Doufan, "we must act. We must also ask, what of you, my ladies?" Doufan addressed the two young women who had remained silent throughout this council in his crowded office.

"I shall go where Lady Fachalana goes," Ansa firmly stated, "and nowhere else."

Fachalana voice came low, barely to be heard, yet still filled with determination. "And I must face my father."

~ ~ ~

"We will not turn you over, sir, no matter what."

"What if my husband orders it?" asked Countess Lomela. It was a question that need be answered.

Sir Corgos was reluctant to provide that answer. "I think, my lady, that if the count so does, then he is no longer competent."

One of the master of arms' lieutenants, standing at his elbow, nodded agreement. "He would have to be under that sorcerer's spell to order such a thing."

"Do it anyway," spoke Donzalo. "Radal's quarrel is with me."

"Oh, no, Master Donzalo. We could never give you to that evil man!" objected Traspa.

The young knight smiled at Lomela's faithful maid. "And I hope you need not. But be prepared if it comes to it. Ah, Sir Jak. How fares my brother?"

The beefy sergeant stood in the doorway, just returned from his visit to the tower.

"The same, Sir Donzalo." He shot an unfriendly look toward Corgos. Jak had most certainly heard their conversation. "Still unwilling to deal with the sorcerer."

"So we remain at stalemate." Donzalo thought of the secret passage he had once used to escape Castle Rosam. Why not take it again? They were all free to move about indoors so he could simply go down a flight of stairs, enter a room, and disappear.

No, he could not abandon those who were here, his brother, the Lady Lomela. But perhaps he should persuade Corgos to take the countess out that way.

"We still have our swords," he said, putting a hand to his own, "so things are not hopeless."

~ ~ ~

"Most of those in the keep are not fighting men but servants and family," Paren said. "It is little wonder that Corgos has not attempted to fight."

"Yet we shall. Are we being rash?" asked Ansa.

"We have no choice."

"Aye, there will come no better time," spoke Sir Blen. "All is readied. My men are gathering in twos and threes, prepared to come together at the gate when it is opened. Over a score and all soldiers of Sharsh whose foremost thought will be to rescue the princess." He looked to the others. "You understand that must be the goal of Lord Doufan and myself."

"And Doufan hides himself in the embassy, committing none of its men to our attack," complained the young woman.

"He can not afford to seem involved if things go awry. 'Tis bad enough that Nafal and I are."

Ansa shrugged and looked to her silent companion. Fachalana was rapt in her own thoughts and was adding nothing to their council. "Where has gone my brother?" she asked.

"Out scouting again," answered Sir Paren. "Sir Oder is certainly one who likes to leave little to chance." Paren suspected that he had been the last to have learned who the Anian was. Or who the woman with whom he spoke was, for that matter.

"Indeed so," agreed Ansa. Who knew where she and her companions fit into her brother's well-laid schemes?

Beside her, Lady Fachalana thought on the words of the Fay, Arsel, and his promise of something that would aid her in the struggle to come, something held by Donzalo. She would know it when the time came, had he promised. What was 'it?' Would it truly help her against all the power of her father? Could she face him at all?

She looked up at the others gathered here in this little cottage and asked, "How much longer must we wait?"

~ ~ ~

Jobareth Nafal led the way along the narrow ledge. It was, of necessity, a slow progress on this moonless night.

Behind him trailed some dozen men, most followers of Sorsen and Mussago who had secretly made their way north in recent days. These looked to the Cuddonian, Habidros, as their leader.

And the brother of Habidros, the minstrel Guesare, made up the last of their party.

Here was the entrance to the cave. "We can chance a lantern, now," said Nafal. Soon, the entire group was inside and began their ascent of the passage below Keep Rosam.

The panel. Where was the catch? Ah, there. He slowly slid it open and stepped through.

There was already a light within the room, and a man — a tall man. "So much for keeping this a secret," said Donzalo Rosam.

17

"There are two men on the wall," whispered Oder. "Whether more stand on the other side of the gate, who can know?"

"I hope to soon find out." Blen felt that any defenders would easily be overwhelmed by his well-trained soldiers, if not slain first by the band of infiltrators. There was, however, another consideration. "Might there be magic barring our way?" He had heard tales of such lately.

"Lady Fachalana sensed none. She feels that Radal would consider an attack here unlikely and not waste his strength by setting a seal." The Anian gazed toward the great oaken gates. "The lady dare not attempt any magic herself, for her father would surely recognize her presence."

"I trust that she will remain safely outside the walls with Sir Paren."

"I would not trust too much."

Behind them their men gathered, ready to rush forward when the gates were opened. A tall fighting man slipped in among them, his face hidden by his basinet, one shoulder rising slightly higher than the other.

~ ~ ~

"We heard that guards ever accompanied you," said Guesare.

"Corgos felt them no longer necessary. Not since Radal seized my brother. I was considering letting him in on this secret way, so he might smuggle out Lomela and the boy. But 'twould be a dangerous undertaking." He looked at the group of fighting men gathered in his former quarters. "Perhaps now, though, it could be a good idea."

"Let us go to her, you and I," said Jobareth, "and to Corgos, as well. These fellows here," he went on, with a nod toward his companions, "intend to open the gates to a larger force."

"Let's go," said Habidros to his men. "Are you with us, Guessy?"

"I would not miss it," said the minstrel. "Good luck to you, my friends."

"Need we avoid guardsmen?" asked Jobareth, once the party of soldiers had slipped out. "Radal's, I mean."

"None of them enter the living quarters. The sorcerer has chosen to keep most close to the tower. Come."

They ascended a stairway. "I suspect that everyone is still together in Lady Lomela's suite," said the young knight. "They were when I left them an hour past."

The door stood open. In a pair of chairs, Sir Jak and the master of arms conversed quietly. The Countess Lomela stood on her balcony, gazing toward the tower where Bolos was prisoner. "It seems the ladies have gone to their beds," remarked Donzalo as they entered.

"Jobareth! How came you here?"

Nafal glaced toward his young companion. "There is a secret way into the castle, my lady," said Donzalo, "which I once showed to our friend Nafal. We think perhaps you and your son should take it now."

"I will not desert my husband. But Sir Jak," she said, turning to the sergeant, "if things here go wrong, I must depend on you to carry Ros to safety. Do this for your count."

"I will, my lady," promised the soldier.

"Follow me," said Donzalo. "I shall show you the way you must take." And then, he thought, I must take a way of my own. "I shall depend on the legate and Sir Corgos to watch over you," he said to the countess and, bowing, departed.

~ ~ ~

Castles are intended to keep men out, not in. Their walls may not be easy to ascend but, if one thinks to bring a suitable length of rope, not difficult to go down.

So down the innermost wall of Keep Rosam went Guesare and the others, and then the second, as well, bypassing the gates and their guardians. Only one other sentry did they spy on the walls and slipped by him easily in the darkness, making their way to the outer fortifications. There, they crept along its lower stone walls, set atop an earthen berm, to the heavy oaken door. Two of Lord Radal's ruffians yawned atop the rampart.

They would open this gate to their compatriots outside. Yes, they could have brought ropes here as well and avoided the gates altogether, but it would have taken longer to bring them all up on a rope or two, and much increased the chance of discovery.

Moreover, if Sorsen and his troop showed up in time, the way would be open to them.

One man went down easily, throat slit without ever seeing his attacker. The other managed to let out a cry of terror before he joined him. Had anyone heard?

It seemed not. The bar was lifted, the gate swung open on its iron hinges.

"Come on in," invited Sir Habidros, beckoning to the waiting men at arms.

Now they needed to breach the other two entries.

~ ~ ~

Dovolo entered. "My lord," said he, "there is aught you should see." He nodded toward the narrow window.

Radal peered into the courtyard below. It was very dark but a pair of torches at the tower entrance allowed him to make out a tall figure, a man standing before the door to Castle Rosam's Great Hall. "Donzalo," he whispered. "At last."

Across that courtyard, Lomela and Jobareth Nafal stood on the lady's balcony. As the young knight stepped forward from the shadows, they spied him as well. "Captain Corgos," called Jobareth. "Donzalo is in the open! We must defend him."

The two men hurried down toward the courtyard, Corgos beckoning to a pair of guardsmen to join them as he went. "You should remain with the countess," he said to Jobareth as they reached the doors. "Watch over her and leave this to me and my men."

Nafal reluctantly agreed and turned about, as the three soldiers stepped out into the moonless night.

Lord Radal's attention must be on me, thought Donzalo, and only me. Not the men even now moving toward him in the darkness.

Above him, Radal saw Corgos and his men. "I must seal the doors over there so none others can interfere. It is but a minor magic." But an inconvenience, thought the sorcerer, as he sent his essence through roundabout ways to a place where he could touch each lock, bind it invisibly.

When satisfied with his craft, he turned to his sergeant and spoke. "The seals I have placed will hold for only a short time. We must finish our work before the garrison can break free.

"Go down and take them. But slay not the Rosam boy; he is mine."

~ ~ ~

There had not even been a guard posted at the second gate. Perhaps Radal had felt the heavy iron portcullis was impassable on its own. Even as it was being opened to Blen and his men, others had reentered the keep by the rope they had left dangling.

Before them in the courtyard, they saw conflict. Four men stood against a crowd of Radal's riff-raff.

"You get the remaining gate," said Guesare to his brother, "and I will aid yon fighters. You come with me," he told one of those who had scaled the wall behind them. The rest followed Habidros along the battlements.

Outnumbered greatly, Donzalo and his comrades were yet a match for their attackers. The first onslaught had left one lying dead before them, and the others had retreated to form a half-ring about the four. Backs quite literally to the wall, swords turned out, they waited.

"So much for sneaking in quietly and rescuing Bolos," sighed Guesare. He and his follower crashed into the rear of the pack without warning. Corgos rushed forward, sword swinging, the others but a step behind him. Radal's men were scattered.

But they were many against few. Ranks were reformed before the tower door. That door opened, to frame Dovolo holding a long dudgeon to the count's throat.

"Surrender," he hissed, "or I'll cut him ear to ear."

Donzalo and Sir Corgos immediately dropped their sword points to the cobbled pavement. The two guards followed their example. Guesare and his companion were not quite so willing to acquiesce.

And from the corner of his eye he could see the rest of his allies coming through the inner gate. It had not been well defended, if at all. Perhaps all this turmoil had drawn its guards away.

Of a sudden, Bolos broke free, in part, and struggled with the man who held him. The dagger flashed and Count Bolos, son of Count Borrago, fell slain in his ancestral home, slain in defense of his brother.

18

Radal slowly climbed to the top of the tower, ready to raise great magics.

Below him, battle raged. What was that he felt? Magic? It must be Guesare trying to lift the seals he had set. Not strong enough.

His staff and his cask were at hand. He must call on those he had never dared before, in this one last act of sorcery, the one that would end his life.

It was not the outcome he would have chosen but one he had ever known might come. And come was the time to raise a wall about himself and the one whom he intended to destroy, the one he hated, to cast him into the deepest of hells.

None could stop it now.

~ ~ ~

Now was battle fully joined.

Though numbers were near equal, the advantage was all to the better trained soldiers who attacked Radal's men. Still, the rabble might be difficult to root out of the defensive position they had taken among pens and outbuildings that lay between tower and castle wall. Moreover, their number included a handful of musketeers. Blen would not have his men charge those gunnes.

This is a good time to try out my bombes, thought the knight. Alas, though he threw the grenade as hard as he might, its glowing fuse a streak of orange through the night, it fell well short of the enemy.

"Would that I had a gunne right now," said Blen, "or even a cata-pult."

"I can give you the latter," said Donzalo, standing nearby. "Have you a lance or even a long stick?"

One of the men found an appropriate length of wood amid the rubble. Donzalo recognized it as a prop for an awning. "Excellent," said he, as he cut a notch a short distance from one end. "Now some leather and lacings." Quickly, he assembled what was unmistakably an oversize sling, which he laced to the end of the pole.

"Place your bombe in the pouch and light the fuse," he ordered, than swung the pole back and snapped it forward with all the force of his tall frame, launching the grenade.

It sailed far and landed amid their opponents. "It is a staff sling," Donzalo told them. "I played with them as a boy."

Habidros looked approvingly upon the results. "On the next one, we will charge."

And they did. It was all sword to sword now. Guesare found himself fighting beside a tall man, a man who seemed familiar.

He dryly commented, "Someday, we must stop helping each other fight our enemies and have our own duel."

Perdos laughed despite himself. Then he saw Dovolo bolt from the fray, hoping to escape a fight his men could not win. "He is mine!" cried he, and pursued the man, sword in hand.

The mercenary leader had clambered up a stairway to the top of the castle wall and now raced along the battlements toward the gate. If he could get beyond it, he might have a chance of disappearing into the night.

But there was no chance of eluding the man who chased him. Dovolo turned to fight, drawing his long sword from the scabbard he wore across his back, and waited.

"Whom do I face?" he asked of the close-helmed man approaching him, heavy blade in hand.

"I am Perdos. I am he who slew Sojel, as I shall slay you."

Dovolo laughed. "I should thank you for Sojel." He launched himself forward with a great overhand cut. Though a shorter man than Perdos, there was strength driving that lengthy blade. Perdos did not remember ever seeing a sword quite so long. Why, one could use it as a lance, he thought, as he parried the blow.

Within a few passes, he realized that the sergeant was an exceptional swordsman. How had the man ended up where he was?

Dovolo chuckled as he deflected a blow from Perdos and nearly brought his own blade through. "You will not beat me, Sir Perdos. Turn away from this fight and I shall as well. I seek only to go."

Allow this murderer of Count Bolos, one of the few man who had always treated him well, to escape? This filth who had ridden with Sojel and taken part in his crimes?

That long blade handicapped the man in close and, especially, down low. Perdos swept his own sword low, hoping the others would follow it. When he did, the knight lunged forward, smashing his shoulder into him, knocking him off balance, before he could bring the long sword up.

Damn! That's my bad shoulder, he thought, but it was worth it. An upward thrust, his blade into Dovolo's unarmored throat, and it was over.

It looked as though the fighting behind him was over too. Should he stay? There would be no duel with Guesare this night and he had done all he could.

As his erstwhile opponent had intended, he slipped out of the castle gate and into the night.

~ ~ ~

Ansa knew her strengths, and fighting battles was not one of them. She had accompanied Lady Fachalana as far as the inner gate — much against the wishes of Sir Paren — but urged her to go no further.

"The fighting is over," said Fachalana. "Come on."

Ansa followed reluctantly into the courtyard.

The minstrel Guesare approached them, blade in hand.

"Where is the castle garrison?" Fachalana asked. "I see only our men."

Guesare smiled inwardly at the 'our.' "Lord Radal's magic has sealed them all within their quarters."

"You can not force them? I heard you had skill in such things."

"These are physical seals," said Guesare. "The ones I placed here before were only to block others' use of magic. This sort requires far more power and are beyond my ability to break." He shrugged. "But it matters little, now, my lady. Your father's troop is defeated and the soldiers of the garrison are unneeded. It is the door to this tower that I must try to open."

Fachalana looked at the door before them and laughed. She could see where the minstrel had clumsily tried to undo the spell.

The lady had practice in unlocking what her father had locked. Had she not often, quite unknowingly, swept aside his seals so she might read his correspondence and books?

What were the proper words? No, not those ones, they were for shattering the door itself. Oh, why didn't she just reach in and — there, it was undone.

She smiled with satisfaction and pushed the door open.

And high above them, Lord Radal noted his daughter's success.

~ ~ ~

"Is it all over?" wondered Lomela.

"Only when Radal is in bonds, my lady," replied Sir Jak. "Best stay off your balcony until then."

The knight stared listlessly from the window. His master's body had been removed, at last. While the fight raged, none could reach it and he had stood here and kept watch over it.

He sighed. Jak blamed no one for what had happened and it was good that the count had gone down fighting, at the last a hero. If only he could have been at his side.

He could tell young Ros that his father was a brave man, when the boy got older.

Sir Jak looked toward the new widow. The Lady Lomela had done well by her husband, hadn't she? All things considered. If she did not grieve over-long, he would understand.

Traspa came to stand beside him. Jak put his arm about his wife and he wept.

~ ~ ~

Guesare bounded up the stairway that wound around the interior of the tower. Radal would surely not give up. He must stop him before he raised magics.

Had this night been success or failure? Yes, Lomela and the boy were safe, and that had been the first concern, but had the death of Bolos been too great a price? Others would have to sort that out.

And there still was very much a danger to Donzalo. The trap door that led to the top floor lay open. The minstrel remembered a council held up here once, a council where Bolos had suggested having nothing more to do with Sharsh. Maybe he had been right.

There stood the sorcerer, staff in one hand, sword in the other.

Guesare held his own blade before him. "Surrender, sir! It is over."

There came a mocking laugh. "It will be over when Donzalo Rosam lies dead." Radal raised his arms and a green light played about him. "Would you hope to best me in sorcery, minstrel?"

"Not if I can use my sword." I could never match his magic, he told himself, and strove to move forward. He was unable.

Well, thought Guesare, it seems I can *not* use my sword, so I must need turn to magic. Might Fachalana be able to help me? The minstrel had never had the gift of the link but attempted to reach out to her.

Standing in the yard below, she felt that touch. Should she turn her power against her own father? Could she help the Cuddonian at all? Fachalana still knew so little!

She did know that she would never be able to establish any sort of link with Guesare. His mind was not made for it. But she might seek to strengthen him, as he employed whatever enchantments he could.

All eyes in that courtyard were lifted to the contest above them, the two men facing each other atop the tower, harsh greenish light rising above the one, the other surrounded by a soft nebulous golden glow.

Guesare spoke a spell. Being a minstrel, words were his strength and the basis for any magic he might attempt.

Mother Rema, darkness confound!
Let Lord Radal now be bound!

THE HAND OF THE SORCERER

Radal felt the invisible bonds placed upon him and shook them away. The fetters had been surprisingly strong. The words he then spoke were of no earthly language, nor can we report them without endangering the reader's soul.

The sorcerer did not bother with any elegance. It was power he unleashed upon Guesare, pure force. The minstrel staggered beneath its blow and attempted to retaliate. He felt another — Fachalana, he assumed — trying to lend him strength.

Lord Radal faltered only a moment before renewing his onslaught. It was hopeless to stand against him. Only steel would stop the man.

Guesare realized that the two had slowly been moving toward each other, step by step. Holding his sword before him, he tried only to withstand the wizard's onslaught long enough to reach him.

Then steel met steel. Radal was no mean swordsman; once, perhaps, he had even been Guesare's equal. He was old now, and worn.

But Guesare, too, was weakened, and the sorcerer continued to attack with both blade and magic. He was moving too slowly, the minstrel knew, missing his chances to get through Lord Radal's guard.

Back and forth across the rough timber floor they battled, the stars of a moonless night blazing above them. Surely others were climbing the stairs by now, thought Guesare, coming to his aid.

His fight, though, had been brief, far briefer than he realized. Men stood only at the bottom of the stairway now, beginning their ascent. Again, Guesare missed with a lunge, awkwardly staggering as the spells of Radal hampered him.

A sword slipped into his side, where his breastplate did not cover, and Sir Guesare slumped, gasping. A second blow ended him.

Far away, Lady Se of Drolwym knew she had lost another child.

~ ~ ~

Fachalana fell to her knees beneath the blow of Guesare's death. How much worse might it have been had they truly linked, both minds in the same space as once she had with her father? She did not think she could survive it.

Ansa knelt, placing her arm about her friend's shoulders. This was not over, she knew. Fachalana would face more, would need all her strength, before ended this night.

And beside them, Oder stood, his face betraying neither his anger nor his grief. Coolly, the Anian nocked an arrow and pulled back his bow.

19

Radal turned his face to the sky, arms outstretched, and called upon his god.

"Asak! I give myself to thee!"

A great dark form rose behind him, above him, from him. Like a web-winged dragon it was, but also some great horned demon-being.

An arrow, flying toward the sorcerer, fell harmlessly upon striking the walls of sickly-green light that surrounded him.

Oder swore, swore by the Great Sky itself. "It is as the shape of Asak, as I have seen him on the altars of his devotees!"

"How can we stand against him?" asked his sister, her voice barely audible.

He looked toward Lady Fachalana. "We must depend on his daughter. Only she can now save Donzalo."

And the walls of sorcery edged outward, threatening soon to enclose all of them within an enchanted circle.

Donzalo looked upward at that shape and remembered another night of the new moon and another battle. He stepped forward, ready to fight again.

~ ~ ~

Should she oppose her father? wondered Fachalana. Might she not join him, stand tall and powerful by his side?

No, came his voice, *you must not. I will not have you damned.*

Then must I fight you? She could not let him harm Donzalo, the man whose destiny she felt was entwined with her own.

But no, she did not love Donzalo, did she? No matter. She would protect him.

Do not stand between me and the Rosam. I do this for you.

He believes that, thought the noblewoman. He is lost to his hatred.

Again she attempted to speak to him, but now she touched only a vast void, icy and alien. Instinctively, Fachalana recoiled from that darkness. It was Asak, she knew, and no longer her father.

She saw the young Laman knight, who now stood closer to tower and wizard-wall than the others, turn to stare at her. Was he thinking of her sister?

"I shall protect you as I can, Sir Donzalo," she promised, even as the walls of sorcerous light engulfed him.

Habidros gasped and attempted to reach his friend. He could not pass, nor could any others who now stood outside that circle. "Blen led men into the tower," said he. "Only they might reach Radal now!"

Fachalana slowly shook her head. "No, they also are barred. Donzalo stands alone." She stretched out a hand toward the barrier, at once like a fire and a mist. It parted before her and she entered.

~ ~ ~

There was trouble up at the keep. Fighting, maybe. Captain Nidanem considered the report for only a moment before making his decision. Yes, his orders were to keep the town safe but he could not stand by if his count needed him.

"One company with me," he told his lieutenant. "You keep the other here on alert." Would that he had a cavalry squadron rather than men at arms. It would take an hour or more to march them to Castle Rosam. It's all uphill, he reminded himself. Push them too hard and they'll be useless for fighting.

As they set forth from their barracks near the ferry-crossing, Nidanem looked toward the keep, set high on its cliffs, and wondered about the greenish light playing above it.

~ ~ ~

Donzalo turned to see the sorcerer's daughter standing at his side. It seemed that great feathered golden wings spread above her, as had once a silver wolf stood over his beloved Jola. He thought of his brooch and his hand went to it.

You will know it when the time comes, had said Arsel. Fachalana recognized the power in the piece of jewelry, the trinket she had seen so often on Donzalo's shoulder, and knew it was that of which Arsel spoke. "Lend me the strength of my sister," she said.

The young knight pinned it to the jack-coat she wore. Did he see a wolf, shadowy, dim, along with the eagle that had taken form?

This is of my sanctuary, Fachalana realized, and she found herself able to draw on the power of that world of silvered horizons, of calm and of peace.

The Shadow-Asak loomed above them, a great black sword in its hand, greenish light flickering along its edges. Donzalo stood with his own blade ready.

Could eagle face dragon? Or, below them, could daughter withstand father — or that which was once her father? Both struggles were one, manifestations of their conflict.

How could he help? The physical Radal was high atop the tower, beyond his reach. Both avatars seemed without substance. That would change, Donzalo knew, and then would that dragon be of danger to him.

And then could he fight it, but he had doubts this ordinary sword he held would harm his enemy. At that moment he wished he held once more the Moon Sword.

That did not keep him from hacking upward at the misshapen, misty creature. It laughed at his attempt.

At least I might distract it, thought Donzalo.

Do not fight me, came a voice, a voice deeper, more melancholy, than Fachalana could ever have thought possible. So filled with despair!

Filled with emptiness, as Brother Grippo had once described Asak to their friend Jobareth.

Join with me! it demanded. *I shall make you mighty, a queen such as the world has never seen.*

No, said another, and she knew it to be what remained of her father. *Do not follow my path.*

Above her, eagle tore at dragon with beak and talon. Would that terrible sword strike her down?

Her strength was not enough.

Seek, said a liquid golden voice. *Seek that which the one beside you once held.*

Fachalana knew without asking that it was her sister, the Jola she had never known, and, yes, the goddess Diba who spoke. And she remembered the sword Donzalo had wielded against her father. She put her hand to the silver wolf above her heart and sought.

Across the silver plain her essence rushed, to the gleaming white temple. Its tall doors opened to her and she beheld the Sword of the Moon, the Prince's Sword.

It was not the sword Donzalo once held in this world, she knew, but a part of it that extended in some manner into that other, even as did sorcerers reach into different worlds. She stepped forward and took its hilt. Such power!

And in this world, the world where she faced what had been her father, she placed her hand upon Donzalo Rosam's sword arm, letting that power flow into him. A silver light played about his blade.

Did Lord Radal, what remained of him, also recognize that power? Did he feel the presence of the daughter he had lost, lending strength to the one that struggled?

Fachalana had let herself be distracted from the fight in this world while searching the other. The eagle was thrown down; she herself staggered before Asak's attack. Donzalo drove his weapon into the form of the ever more corporeal demon.

A hiss of anger and the great black sword swung, barely missing the knight as he threw himself back to avoid its sweep.

He could not long escape that blade. And Fachalana was reeling, barely holding on, but the eagle rose again to the attack on wings of golden fire.

Had Donzalo truly wounded their enemy? Around them, the wizard wall flickered and sparked, silver and green contending, shifting, beneath the dark sky.

~ ~ ~

"It is weakened! Perhaps now may our missiles penetrate the barrier," spoke Oder.

205

THE HAND OF THE SORCERER

Habidros raised his brother's rifle to his shoulder and took aim. Did his bullet strike the sorcerer? He was not sure but it seemed that the figure flinched.

An arrow flew from Oder's recurved bow. Another followed, as the Cuddonian hurried to reload.

He looked up. "I'm sure he is hit," he said, as he spanned the clockwork firing mechanism of his weapon. Habidros primed the rifle and raised it to fire again.

Then he lowered it. The shadow demon above Radal had grown vast, hiding the stars. Its voice came as the inchoate howling of mountain winds, while its clawed hands tore at the great eagle that struggled in its grip.

There stood the sorcerer yet. Habidros took aim and fired, even as Oder released another shaft.

As a madman, Donzalo hewed at the creature that loomed above him, supporting the exhausted Lady Fachalana with his other arm. Weary though she was, she fought on. Both fought on.

~ ~ ~

Let my arrow fly true, prayed Oder, once more drawing his bow. Beside him, his sister Ansa said her own prayers for the two trapped behind the sorcerous wall, the two for whom she cared above all others.

Above them yet stood the sorcerer, Lord Radal, his staff in one hand, the other reaching toward the skies. A flame seemed to surround him, a green fire that burned coldly.

He faltered. All around, the wall of light was collapsing in a chaos of silver and green, of flame and darkness and tumult. The ground trembled.

Then Radal was falling, falling in fire, falling to his final ruin. Was he stricken or had he, at the last, chosen to leap?

And Fachalana was falling even as did her father.

OF DESTINY: THE LAST TALE

1

Hooves thundered as a company of men rode to the outer gates of Castle Rosam. A hint of peach-colored light above the hills spoke of the coming dawn.

A troop in the Rosam colors stood guard at those gates. Their leader held up a hand. "Sir Sorsen! I was told you might show up, my lord."

Sorsen spoke to the man from horseback. "Captain Nidanem, isn't it? How fares it here?"

"It is all over, sir. I was told to let you and your men in." The officer turned toward the keep's entrance. "Open for them, lads," he called to the guards. Turning back, he said, "Best I let Captain Corgos give you all the news."

Sorsen and Mussago passed through the other two gates, their men behind them, and into the courtyard. There seemed to be a cleanup in progress, after whatever action the night had seen. They noted the bodies laid out on one side of the area.

Corgos stood speaking to Sir Paren as they oversaw the work. "Ho!" called Paren, upon spying them. "Too late for the fighting, sirs, but you might help us tidy up."

"What of Lord Radal?" asked Sorsen, dismounting.

"Dead, sir," spoke Sir Corgos. "As, alas, is the count."

"As well as Sir Guesare," added Paren.

"Ah, Guesare. He was a good man." *I may have to give the news to his brother Galaro next spring,* thought Orgelo's son.

"May Kamat grant them rest," said Mussago. Then, ever practical, he inquired, "Who governs County Rosam?"

Paren considered that question for a moment. "I suppose Countess Lomela and myself will have to act for little Ros. Perhaps

Donzalo too, if he is willing. And," he went on, looking to the pair of southerners, "if there is no objection from the other counties."

"My father would agree with this, I am certain," responded Sorsen. "That is probably the only voice that matters." He glanced sidelong at his companion. Mussago did not rise to the bait.

"But now you must tell us all of what happened here."

"Jobareth Nafal could do that. He is within with the Lady Lomela. But," asked Sir Paren, "could you first lend us some of your men to help out here? There are many dead to give to the fire."

~ ~ ~

That which had been Lord Radal, a twisted, charred remnant, had been wrapped in cloth of cotton. "I will see that he is returned to Sharsh, " Jobareth Nafal told the sorcerer's daughter. She gave no sign of having heard him.

She is damaged, thought Jobareth, and I know not whether it can be undone. Fachalana sat enrapt, barely acknowledging those about her.

Sir Blen, when able, stayed by her side. Ansa rarely left it.

Pinned to her gown was Donzalo's wolf brooch. "It should remain with her," said he. "It may lend her strength." He, of all those who cared for the lady, most knew that she needed it, that it might be the anchor to keep her from drifting from them forever.

Donzalo also knew where she must go to find a cure, for she had whispered to him after their fight, and spoken no words since to any other.

"I must dream."

~ ~ ~

"I think, Countess Lomela, that I may soon be withdrawn as ambassador." Doufan nodded somewhat in the direction of Jobareth. "The legate here should do well enough without me."

Lomela also looked toward her lifelong friend. "Are you going to tell him, Jobareth?

"Sir," the young diplomat began, with a tone that held a certain defensiveness. "I intend to resign from the diplomatic corps and serve the countess."

"Ah! I fear our Blen will not appreciate once again being left in charge," chuckled Lord Doufan. "I shall not attempt to dissuade you from this. In truth, boy, I think it is an excellent decision. But don't tell your grandfather I so said!"

Jobareth appeared relieved. *The boy values my approval*, thought the ambassador. *It will be good to have such a friend in Castle Rosam.* He considered the young Lady Lomela for a moment. *And perhaps in the countess' bed*, he mentally added.

"Blen and I must travel before we do aught else," Jobareth stated. "We accompany Sir Donzalo."

"And the Anian and Habidros, carrying Sir Gusare's remains to the Cuddon." Doufan nodded slowly. "You must both go?"

"It is not only Guesare we take but also Lady Fachalana," replied Jobareth. "Donzalo is certain it is the only remedy for her wounds."

Lord Doufan digested this information briefly. "We must do what we can for the lady. An unimaginable debt is owed her.

"I do not expect to leave immediately, Nafal. Indeed, I may well remain a season or three. Take your time."

But he had done what could be done in Lama and, sooner or later, he would leave. There was little left to accomplish here.

And Aulla's husband — a rather dangerous looking ruffian, thought Doufan — did not much approve of him swiving his wife.

~ ~ ~

"There is an empty keep I know in the Cuddon," spoke Donzalo, with a wink to Oder. "It might just be the place to take up residence one of these days."

The lad seemed little the worse for the fight he had just been in, bruised some in body, but undamaged in spirit. He mourned Guesare, of course, as did the Anian.

"First, though," he said, "we must take home our friend. And the Lady Fachalana, too, I believe should travel with us."

"When?" Oder saw little point in lingering longer in County

Rosam. Though he did have his sister to consider — she might keep him longer.

"My brother's funeral is on the morrow. Then, perhaps." Another the boy would mourn, a brother who had followed their father into death.

Guesare's coffin awaited its journey to Drolwym, containing a body charred beyond any recognition. In those final minutes of Lord Radal's existence, all atop the tower had burned. There was a sizable hole through the floor up there. Paren would eventually see to its repair, assumed Donzalo. He had no great desire to take up such responsibilities here.

But he could see himself putting Sabatare's old keep to right. It was a good spot, and not that far from here. Yes, he could see himself there and he could see one standing beside him.

That was the sort of destiny of which he approved.

~ ~ ~

"I must take care of my brother," said Habidros. "As soon as I may, I shall ride back to Tod-ford."

"My cousin will be disappointed," remarked Sorsen.

"Lenasha would like the Cuddon," Habidros responded, "and they appreciate such women there. She must meet my family eventually!"

"I could not see Thane Vantare ever traveling to County Arvaram," laughed Donzalo, "so I suppose it would be necessary to take your bride to him."

"Take care, my friend. And take care of that rifle." Guesare's gunne now hung in its richly worked scabbard from his brother's saddle. "I hear it has done good work for you." Sorson mounted, surveyed Castle Rosam one last time.

Habidros agreed. "I still insist that it was my bullet that ended Radal, and not the Anian's arrow!"

Donzalo was not convinced that it was either but, rather, the dark sorcerer's choice at the end not to allow his daughter's destruction. But who could ever say? He spoke not of it, nor ever again of that night.

"Then we bid all of Castle Rosam a farewell," said Sir Sorsen, turning his horse. The taciturn Mussago saluted them and both rode from the keep, their men following.

Habidros waved once more before they disappeared through the arch of the gate.

"Do you think those two lordlings have become friends?" asked Donzalo of Sir Blen.

"We will know better when both become counts," Blen answered, shrugging. "They can afford to be friendly now."

2

"Sir Copago! Hail! Who are these who ride with you?"

"Friends of Donzalo I met on the road. We were both headed here." He dismounted to take the hand of Sir Corgos. "I hear that we are far too late for all that happened."

"Very true," said one master of arms to the other, "but you have come just soon enough that you did not miss Sir Donzalo's departure."

"Where is the boy?" asked a bear-like man who had come to stand beside them.

"Over in the stables, I think." Corgos tipped his head in that direction. "I can only assume that you are a brother of Galaro and Habidros."

"That I am, sir. I am Mausare."

"And I, Sir Corgos. What brought you all the way from the upper Cuddon?"

"My father sent me," the burly Cuddonian replied and started off in the direction the knight had indicated.

"They had some inkling of the trouble brewing here and the Thane of Drolwym had them ride." Copago looked toward the broad back of the man walking from them. "This Mausare has, like Habidros, been a captain of mercenaries so he was chosen to lead them. He seems a good fellow, though given to moods."

Corgos turned to regard the man, as well. "I think I shall accompany our Mausare. You can find lodgings on your own I am most certain, Sir Copago." He followed after the Cuddonian.

Donzalo was busied with the loading of a cart and saw not the man who approached him.

"Is this my brother?" asked Mausare in a quiet, even voice, looking upon the long box that was being carefully stowed.

"It is, Cousin," said Donzalo, embracing the man.

"It is good to see you, boy, despite the circumstances. And Oder!" The Anian had stepped forward from where he stood in shadow. "I've not beheld you in years." His smile came bitter-sweet. "I rejoice that there was a bard to chronicle Guesare's final battle."

"The events are still too close for me to compose a lay. In time."

"I understand this," said Mausare. He spoke again to Donzalo. "I have messages from Lady Se, but I suppose you can guess what is in them."

"She wishes me to bring the Lady Fachalana so the Fay might aid her, even as they did Jola."

"And as they did you."

Corgos had come up behind the Cuddonian. "Will you accompany Sir Donzalo and his party back to your homeland?"

"So do I intend," replied Mausare. "We were sent to fetch him."

"Then enjoy our hospitality for a day or two. We would not have you return weary to the road." He looked toward Oder and Donzalo. "You do not mind the delay, gentlemen?"

"Not I," replied the youthful knight. "Mausare and I have much catching up to which we must attend!"

~ ~ ~

There was a donkey cart on the street, laden with Mistress Rassana's modest belongings. I'll make that Dame Rassana soon, she told herself, and have Dorbi stand beside me before a priest. She did not think that would prove difficult.

"Ready?" asked Perdos.

"I always was," she answered.

The knight took a long look toward the Keep Rosam, standing above the city. It was time for a farewell to this place, maybe for good.

As he had said farewell to Bolos on the yesterday. He had attended the count's funeral and none had stayed him. Perdos shook the reins and the donkey started forward; his horse was tied behind and followed.

I'll need more horses at the inn, he thought. He had always felt that it would be good country for raising them, down-river where they were headed. Maybe good for raising a houseful of brats, too, Perdos mused, taking a look at the woman seated beside him.

And farewell to Sir Guesare. He no longer found it in himself to hate the man. Perhaps he hadn't for some time. Guesare had died a brave man and by another hand than his own. So be it and may his shade find rest.

Perhaps in some afterworld, the minstrel and his brother Percos could have another go at each other. Perdos smiled at that thought, as the cart followed the Great Road south and out of Ros-town.

~ ~ ~

"I suppose I needn't have called for you," Lareth told his son. "Things have settled down in Lama and now we can both go home, long before winter sets in."

"Sire, will Lomela be all right?" Gawis had never been close to his much younger sister but certainly wished her no ill. He seemed as restless as ever to his father, pacing back and forth. Maybe he just wants to get back to his wife, Lareth thought.

"Perhaps better than before. The loss of Count Bolos was no great blow to anyone, though I hear that he died well." The king gazed a while into the fire. "Lomela has competent friends to stand beside her. Jobareth Nafal, not the least of them."

"He is leaving our service, I hear."

"I always had doubts about that boy as a career diplomat. Far too independent." He thought of another too independent man who had served him and then banished that thought. "Lord Doufan will return to us soon," he went on. "We need him more here in Sharsh than they do in Lama. And there will be one with him, a Sir Blen, for whom I have expectations. You should make his acquaintance, Gawis."

The prince smirked. "I have thought of stealing Modareth's protege, Sir Pol, from him. He is also a man for whom one should have expectations."

"A talented lad, from all I have heard. I doubt he will want to serve Modi in Dor."

"Not with his successes in Celatas, sir."

"Should he continue those successes, he will not wish to serve anyone, my boy."

~ ~ ~

"We shall stop a while at your manor, Uncle, as it is on our way. Then, on up the road and into the Cuddon."

"Say hello to my mother," said Grippo, seated in the corner, where he had been dealing with a rather large pastry. He had resumed his robes of an acolyte and should receive his postponed priesthood this coming year. He was still not positive it was what he wanted.

"*Our* mother," corrected Copago, "and to my wife as well."

"We'll all see our loved ones soon," Sir Paren said, "There's little reason for us to remain much longer at Keep Rosam.

"Donni, are you sure it's a good idea to go into the hills at this time of year?"

"Another month and we might see some hard going." Donzalo thought back to his previous journey there. "I am assured it won't be bad now." His expression went from the light-hearted to the serious. "And I think the Lady Fachalana should wait no longer."

He rose, his head coming perilously close to the ceiling beams. "It's to bed for me. I want to get an early start."

3

It had been a rugged way, traveling up the backbone of the Cuddon, but the mild autumn weather had held.

"We missed Harvest Feast back home," Donzalo informed Sir Blen, who rode beside him.

"I wonder if I shall be in Lama when next it comes," replied the knight. "Our friend Jobareth, it seems, intends to remain permanently."

"I know not where I shall be in a year, either. Perhaps in this land through which we now ride."

Blen looked out across the colorless hills. "The Cuddon would not be my choice, Sir Donzalo. Lord Doufan has hinted that I shall accompany him to Sharsh when he returns. Perhaps I shall go down the River Chas a way and see if anything has changed."

Mausare came up to join them. "The turn is near," he said. Donzalo nodded and looked back to the cart where rode the Lady Fachalana. Ansa sat by her side as she had every day of this journey and, indeed, every day since her soul had been blasted.

Ahead lay Mausare's home, Guesare's home, but they would turn aside here.

They would have to tend to Fachalana before they beheld the haphazard towers of Drolwym Keep.

~ ~ ~

It was to be his tragedy, Sir Pol had told her. He had moved it up to mid-season, to make way for a different closer. Pol was secretive about that but rumor had it the closer would be Jobareth Nafal's long-delayed "Oemse."

It did not seem that Viscountess Fachalana would ever reclaim her theater and Nafal had apparently decided to remain in Lama. Mara did not know either very well.

She idly tapped out a tune on the dulcimer, one of the dances of Narcles. Did he still compose for her father's court? Mara put down her hammers and let her hands slide over the ornate instrument, its richly-hued mahogany sides carved with creatures of the sea. It was the most treasured of all the possessions she had brought with her from her home.

Mara had dreamed again of home, but it was a peaceful dream. The princess had walked beside the sea and another walked with her. Perhaps, she thought, it had been her father, that weak, indulgent man, or perhaps it had been some other. Mara had awakened suddenly, wondering, from that idyll.

The old priest had been right. These dreams were but phantoms of her own mind, embodiments of her fears, of her hopes. Gawis had awakened when she stirred and had held her in his arms until she returned to sleep.

Gawis had returned to her. That was all that mattered, she told herself. Gawis was returned and they would attend the theater this night. It was time that she readied herself.

Which gown would best conceal her ever more obvious pregnancy from the eyes of the crowd? That she was with child was common knowledge but there was no sense in displaying it — and it did show with Mara's slender body. Perhaps that stiff, heavily embroidered dress of cream-colored silk would do. Its rigidity had ever annoyed her but could be an asset tonight. And the weather was cool enough for an enveloping cape.

The princess smiled. She couldn't get away with that in her tropical homeland.

That homeland was the past. Sharsh was Mara's home now and, if Kamat were willing, she carried its future king within her.

Mara busied herself with thinking of names for that king as she dressed.

~ ~ ~

Before them stood the hill of the Fay. The Cuddonian retainers had remained a distance back as the comrades approached its entrance.

Fachalana stood erect, turning her head slowly from side to side as if seeking. She senses what lies here, thought Donzalo.

He looked up to the overcast sky, the ever-shifting sky of the

Cuddon, and then to the pine-clad hills. Did he spy a horse of dappled gray running there?

"The entrance is before us," he whispered to the others, "if you look properly."

There was one coming from it, his snow-white face framed by raven hair.

"Arsel. I greet you," spoke Donzalo, stepping forward.

"And I you, Donzalo. So destiny has led you back to us." The fay surveyed the group. "Only he who loves her may enter with the Lady Fachalana," stated the prince.

The eyes of Oder and Jobareth, Mausare and Habidros, turned to Donzalo, but not those of Ansa. The young Laman slowly bowed his head toward Sir Blen.

"I am he," said the knight of Sharsh and, taking Fachalana's arm, followed Prince Arsel into the halls of the Fay.

Ansa sighed deeply. Donzalo put his arm around her and said, "Let us take Guesare home."

AFTERWORD

I hope you have enjoyed this, the fourth and final book in the saga of *Donzalo's Destiny*. So concludes the story of young Donzalo and his friends, though we may revisit their world one day.

This fantasy novel is set in a place and time of its own, although it most closely resembles 16th Century Central Europe. The stories and characters, the world in which they "exist," arise from ideas I have played with for many years.

Incidentally, if one wishes to pronounce the names in this book, it is generally safe to treat them as one would Spanish — at least the names that come from the widely-spoken Muram language.

Stephen Brooke

Author and artist Stephen Brooke lives and works in an old farmhouse in the Florida Panhandle. *The Hand of the Sorcerer* is his eleventh book.

All are available from Arachis Press, a small publisher dedicated to presenting meaningful literature for readers of all ages. Visit http://arachispress.com for our catalog.